A VERY SPECIAL LOVE

Barbara Cartland

Barbara Cartland Ebooks Ltd

This edition © 2020

ISBNs

9781788672511   EPUB

9781788672528   PAPERBACK

Book design by M-Y Books
m-ybooks.co.uk

THE BARBARA CARTLAND ETERNAL COLLECTION

The Barbara Cartland Eternal Collection is the unique opportunity to collect all five hundred of the timeless beautiful romantic novels written by the world's most celebrated and enduring romantic author.

Named the Eternal Collection because Barbara's inspiring stories of pure love, just the same as love itself, the books will be published on the internet at the rate of four titles per month until all five hundred are available.

The Eternal Collection, classic pure romance available worldwide for all time .

THE LATE DAME BARBARA CARTLAND

Barbara Cartland, who sadly died in May 2000 at the grand age of ninety eight, remains one of the world's most famous romantic novelists. With worldwide sales of over one billion, her outstanding 723 books have been translated into thirty six different languages, to be enjoyed by readers of romance globally.

Writing her first book 'Jigsaw' at the age of 21, Barbara became an immediate bestseller. Building upon this initial success, she wrote continuously throughout her life, producing bestsellers for an astonishing 76 years. In addition to Barbara Cartland's legion of fans in the UK and across Europe, her books have always been immensely popular in the USA. In 1976 she achieved the unprecedented feat of having books at numbers 1 & 2 in the prestigious B. Dalton Bookseller bestsellers list.

Although she is often referred to as the 'Queen of Romance', Barbara Cartland also wrote several historical biographies, six autobiographies and numerous theatrical plays as well as books on life, love, health and cookery. Becoming one of Britain's most popular media personalities and dressed in her trademark pink, Barbara spoke on radio and television about social and political issues, as well as making many public appearances.

In 1991 she became a Dame of the Order of the British Empire for her contribution to literature and her work for humanitarian and charitable causes.

Known for her glamour, style, and vitality Barbara Cartland became a legend in her own lifetime. Best remembered for her wonderful romantic novels and loved by millions of readers worldwide, her books remain treasured for their heroic heroes, plucky heroines and traditional values. But above all, it was Barbara Cartland's overriding belief in the positive power of love to help, heal and improve the quality of life for everyone that made her truly unique.

AUTHOR'S NOTE

Girls are usually accepted into a Convent at the age of eighteen.

A girl first becomes a Postulant for nine months, then a novice for two years and it is then, if they still feel that they have heard 'The Call', they take their final vows at a mystical Religious Ceremony.

Vowing to forsake all others, they become a 'Bride of Christ' and are given a gold Wedding ring often shaped like a crucifix.

Once they have taken their vows they rarely leave the Order that they have committed themselves to.

But a few who have done so have married, had children and written a book about their experiences.

CHAPTER ONE
1869

The Marquis of Okehampton felt sleepy.

It was not surprising considering that he had for two hours with an insatiable expertise been making love to the beautiful Yasmin Caton.

She was, he thought, one of the most passionate women he had ever met, besides being one of the loveliest.

At the same time enough was enough and, while he thought that it would be an effort to move, he had a sudden longing to be on his way home to his house in Park Lane.

He stirred preparatory to climbing out of bed and Yasmin, who was close against him, said in a low voice,

"I have something to tell you, Rayburn."

The Marquis made a sound that was hardly a question and she continued,

"I heard only this afternoon from Paris that Lionel has collapsed with a very severe stroke."

The Marquis stiffened.

"This afternoon?" he exclaimed. "And you entertained me here at dinner tonight?"

"I told nobody and I was so looking forward to seeing you."

The Marquis was silent in sheer astonishment.

Lord Caton was an extremely distinguished man who was of great importance to the Queen and had gone to Paris on a special mission to meet with the Emperor of France.

He was, although it seemed incredible, forty years older than his wife.

All the more then, if he had suffered from a stroke, as Yasmin had just told him, she should undoubtedly now be at his side.

As if she guessed what he was thinking, Lady Caton said,

"Naturally I am leaving for Paris first thing tomorrow morning, but I had to see you, Rayburn, I *had* to!"

"Then, if you are leaving early – " the Marquis began.

He would have moved away from her, but she put her hand on his chest to prevent him from doing so, saying as she did,

"I have something else to tell you."

"What is it?" he asked.

"I am going to have a baby!"

The Marquis was stunned into silence.

"What we have to do, dearest," Yasmin Caton went on, "is to wait until Lionel dies, which according to the letter I have just received will not be long, then be married secretly perhaps in France."

The Marquis thought that he could not be hearing her aright, as she continued,

"Then we can go on a long, long honeymoon before we announce that our marriage has taken place several months previously. Although the child will be born prematurely, there will be no question of it not being yours."

The Marquis was still speechless as she moved closer to him and said in a caressing voice,

"Then we will be very happy, dearest, and when I am your wife all my dreams will come true!"

The Marquis was aware that a great number of women had thought that if they could marry him it would indeed be the dream of their lives.

But he had no intention of marrying anybody, least of all a woman who he was having an *affaire de Coeur* with.

There had been many women in his life, which was not surprising, considering that he was not only extremely handsome and attractive but one of the wealthiest men in England.

Ever since he had left Oxford University he had been pressured towards marriage.

His relatives had almost gone down on their knees to beseech him to settle down and have an heir.

He had been absolutely determined that nobody, definitely nobody, should choose his wife for him.

He was not at all sure exactly what he wanted, but it was certainly not a woman who in becoming his mistress had been unfaithful to her husband.

His contemporaries in the smart Social world that he lived in and relished would have laughed at him for having such ideas.

It was the Prince of Wales who had made easy it for the first time for a gentleman to have an affair with a woman of his own class.

His Royal Highness's interest in the Princesse de Sagan and other beautiful women had naturally caused a great deal of comment. It had altered the rules of Society, which, while unwritten, were invariably obeyed by those who were accepted socially.

The Marquis had therefore made love to the lovely women who attracted him without his behaviour being considered in any way outrageous.

He had thought that Yasmin Caton was one of the most beautiful creatures he had ever seen.

From the very first moment when they had been introduced, there had been a vibration between them that made it inevitable what the outcome would be.

At least that was what he had thought, but now it appeared from what Yasmin had just said that the story was by no means at an end.

He was not only astounded by what she had told him but horrified.

The Marquis had been in many dangerous situations in his life, but it flashed through his mind that this was more dangerous than anything he had ever encountered before.

Bullets had missed him by a hair's breadth and by a miracle his life had been saved at sea.

He knew now that another miracle was needed if he was to escape from a trap that he would be a prisoner in for the rest of his life.

The Marquis was astute and very quick-witted, but for the moment he felt as if his head was filled with cotton wool and he was finding it difficult to know what to say or think.

How could he have imagined for one moment that Yasmin Caton would contrive to force him to marry her?

She had put him in a position where it would be impossible for him to refuse to make what the servants called 'an honest woman' of her.

His first thought was that perhaps things were not as bad as she had thought and Lord Caton would not die.

Then he knew, if he was honest, that the last time he had seen his Lordship at Windsor Castle he had thought that he looked drawn and tired and even older than he actually was.

The Marquis strove wildly to find words to answer Yasmin with, but before he could do so she said,

"I love you, Rayburn, I love you with all my heart and, as I know that you love me, what could be more wonderful than that I should give you a son?"

She spoke in a gushing voice that he thought now he had heard her use before on several occasions and had considered it far too effusive.

Then, almost as if he was being helped by some power beyond himself, a conversation came back to him.

It had taken place soon after he had first met Yasmin Caton.

He remembered sitting in White's Club in St. James's with one of his special friends whom he had served with in the same Regiment.

His name was Harry Blessington and they had been discussing the next house party that the Marquis was to give at Oke Castle, his magnificent ancestral home in Sussex.

He seldom gave a party without Harry being present, especially when it was one that included the London beauties who they were both interested in.

Slowly, as if he was feeling his way through dark clouds, the Marquis made himself recall what had been said.

"I suppose you are asking Yasmin Caton?" Harry Blessington had asked. "I saw you with her last night."

"She is unusually beautiful," he had answered.

"I agree with you and my mother, who knows her family well, has often claimed that it was a crime to make a girl who was so lovely marry a man old enough to be her father."

"I suppose, as Caton is rich and prestigious, they considered that was all that mattered," he replied cynically.

"Of course," Harry agreed, "and they rushed Yasmin up to the Altar before she was even eighteen and obviously had no idea what a crashing bore Caton could be!"

"I have hardly ever spoken to him."

"I had him next to me for two hours the other night at a dinner at Windsor Castle," Harry grumbled, "and he droned on until I thought I should go mad!"

"In which case," he recalled saying with a twist of his lips, "I must obviously console his wife."

"He married again to have an heir," Harry had told him reflectively, "as his first wife only produced daughters, but my mother told me that once again he has been frustrated."

The Marquis had not been listening to Harry with much attention, but now he was sure that Harry had finished by saying,

"The beautiful Yasmin had a bad fall out hunting a year after they were married and that apparently put paid to any hopes she might have of producing a son!"

While giving only one ear to Harry's story, the Marquis was thinking just how beautiful Yasmin Caton was.

He was also planning how he would have the opportunity of telling her so very much more eloquently than he could do in words.

Now, like a light in the darkness, what Harry had told him came flooding back.

He knew now that Yasmin was trying yet another trick on him and, God knows, he had encountered quite a number of them to force him up the aisle.

The numbness that had encompassed him and muddled his brain now vanished.

He could think clearly, he was after all not trapped, and his one idea was to get away without a scene.

Aloud he said to her,

"I think you are looking too far ahead. What you have to do now, Yasmin, is to leave for Paris and hope that nobody is ever aware that I dined with you after you received the letter telling you of your husband's sudden illness."

"I have locked it away in my jewel case," Yasmin replied.

The Marquis only hoped that her lady's maid would not have any opportunity of reading it.

Aware how servants always gossiped, he recognised that a story like this would circulate round Mayfair quicker than the North wind.

"You are very sensible," he said to her, "but now I must leave you."

Yasmin tried to hold onto him, but he rose from the bed and started to dress.

As if she thought that it was necessary for him to recognise how beautiful she was, she lay back against the pillows her body looking, as he had told her earlier, as translucent as a pearl.

As the Marquis adjusted his tie in the mirror over the mantelpiece, he could see her very clearly behind him.

He was thinking now that she was not beautiful but merely dangerous.

He had never been foolish enough to think that she was a clever woman, but he had not realised that she was such a determined one.

He could now understand that, if she was debarred from enjoying all social activities for a year while she was in mourning for her husband, she would realise that she might easily lose him.

She had therefore thought out the only way that she could make him feel completely and absolutely beholden to her.

If, as she was planning, they were married within a month or two or perhaps even sooner, there would be no reason for him to learn until some time later that the baby was just a myth of her over-active mind.

The Marquis shrugged himself into his long-tailed evening coat as he walked to the side of the bed.

Yasmin held out her arms, but he knew if he kissed her that she would pull him down on top of her and once again it would be hard to escape.

Instead he took both her hands in his, kissing first one and then the other.

"Take care of yourself, Yasmin," he said in his deep voice.

"You will think of me, dearest wonderful Rayburn?" she asked. "You know that I will be counting the hours until I see you again."

The Marquis did not answer.

He only moved towards the door and, as he opened, it Yasmin cried,

"Wait! I have something else to say – "

She was too late.

The door closed before her sentence was half-finished and she could hear the Marquis moving quickly down the thickly carpeted stairs to the front door.

Outside his carriage was waiting and, as soon as he appeared, the footman jumped down from the box to open the carriage door.

He was a little earlier than usual and he had been half-afraid that his carriage might not yet have arrived.

Unlike many of his contemporaries, he was extremely considerate towards his servants.

If he knew that he was not likely to be leaving the house where he was dining much before two o'clock, he would order his carriage accordingly.

It always irritated him to know that his coachman and his horses were waiting outside and resenting the fact that they were kept out so late.

Now, as he stepped into his carriage, the footman put a light rug over his knees.

The Marquis thought to himself as he did so that like a fox he was running to ground and there were just a very few seconds to save himself from being torn to pieces by the hounds.

How could he have imagined that Yasmin Caton would sink so low as to try to deceive him with the oldest trick in the world?

If it had not been for Harry Blessington's mother, he would be in an impossible position.

He would have had to agree to Yasmin's insistence that he should marry her the moment she was free.

A lesser man might have refused to do so because the child was her husband's in the eyes of the Law.

But that, the Marquis knew, would be at the expense of betraying his every instinct of how a gentleman should behave.

It was something that would make him ashamed of himself for being what the members of White's would undoubtedly call a 'bounder'.

Women could cheat and no one thought the worse of them. In fact as one wit had said,

"No lady has to be a gentleman!"

But the unwritten laws of being a gentleman were very strict and any man who broke them was liable to be thrown out of his Club and ostracised by his friends.

At the same time, when he reached his house in Park Lane, the Marquis had to face the fact that he was not yet entirely out of the woods.

If Lord Caton died, and it seemed inevitable that he soon would, Yasmin would surely continue to try to deceive him.

Although he had avoided a scene tonight by not telling her what he suspected to be the truth, there would inevitably be scenes and flaming rows in the future.

The whole scenario made him shudder.

If there was one thing that the Marquis really disliked it was tears and recriminations from a woman he was no longer interested in.

It always meant cries of 'why do you no longer love me?'

'What have I done to lose you?' and

'How can you be so cruel?'

It made him feel as if he would never be able to show any interest in a woman again for the rest of his life.

And yet inevitably a few days later he would see another lovely woman and be aware of the invitation in her eyes and the provocative pout on her lips.

Then he would feel once again the first warmth of desire and know that sooner or later she would end up in his arms.

"The real trouble with you, Rayburn," Harry had said to him once, "is that you are too damned good-looking!"

The Marquis had laughed.

"That is hardly my fault!"

"Your father was one of the best-looking men I have ever seen," Harry had gone on, "and your mother was lovely. I can understand how he found it difficult to find anybody to take her place although there must have been plenty of applicants."

'That was true,' the Marquis thought now.

When his valet had helped him undress and, when he had climbed into bed, he found himself thinking of his mother rather than Yasmin.

When she had died, she was still beautiful even though her hair was white and her face was lined.

As a young girl she had been breathtakingly lovely, but it was not only her beauty that mattered, the Marquis thought, it was because she was so sweet, gentle and loving.

What was more he was quite certain that the only man who had ever touched her had been his father.

She would no more have thought of being unfaithful to him than of flying to the moon!

'How could I possibly contemplate marrying someone like Yasmin, beautiful though she is?' he asked himself, 'and have to wonder how many men sitting at my table have been her lovers or are likely to become so?'

At the same time the *debutantes* he had met, and there were not many, seemed gauche, plain and usually painfully shy.

They had, of course, been paraded in front of him whenever their ambitious Mamas had the chance at balls and house parties where the hostess had an unmarried daughter and even at dinner parties too.

He would find himself seated next to a girl of eighteen and know exactly why she was his dinner partner.

How could he ever marry someone, however suitable from a worldly point of view, who would bore him stiff from the moment he put a ring on her finger?

His thoughts were once again on Yasmin and before he went to sleep he made up his mind if possible never to see her again.

He was quite certain that she would bombard him with her letters, but that was nothing unusual.

If and when Lord Caton died, they were not likely to run into each other at any party because for a year, following the example set by Queen Victoria, she would have to forgo all social activities.

*

When the Marquis was called at eight o'clock the following morning, he felt as if, after a terrible nightmare the night before, that the sun was now shining.

He went down to breakfast in a buoyant mood.

Then, almost as if the ghost of Yasmin was still haunting him, he had a sudden longing for the country.

He knew that today he was supposed to have luncheon with the Prince of Wales and tonight there was a dinner party for a ball where he would meet his special friends and many of the beauties who were captivating the Social world at the moment.

He had the feeling that every beautiful woman would look to him like Yasmin and he would be suspicious that beneath the surface there were lurking lies, deceptions and danger.

'I will go to the country,' the Marquis decided firmly.

He rose from the breakfast table and walked into his study, which was an attractive room overlooking a small garden at the back of the house.

He knew as he did so that the butler would notify his secretary where he was and his secretary would bring his letters to him there.

Mr. Barrett was an elderly man, who had been with his father during the last years of his life and his staying on was the chief reason that the Marquis's estates were run so well.

His houses were kept stocked with excellent staff and his engagements carefully detailed so that none was ever forgotten.

The Marquis had already seated himself at his flat-topped Georgian writing desk when Mr. Barrett came into the room.

"Good morning, my Lord," he said respectfully. "I am afraid I have rather more letters today than usual."

As he spoke, he placed two piles down on the desk, one the Marquis knew were private letters that Mr. Barrett was too discerning to open.

The other and larger pile was of invitations and appeals from charities, which ran into an astronomical number during the year.

"Is there anything pressing here, Barrett?" the Marquis asked.

"No more than usual, my Lord, except that there is a Priest here who wishes to see you."

"A Priest?" the Marquis asked. "Begging, I suppose! Surely you can deal with him?"

"He has called, my Lord, regarding Miss Zia Langley."

The Marquis stared at him as for a moment as he could not place the name.

Then he asked,

"Do you mean Colonel Langley's daughter?"

"Yes, my Lord. You will remember that she is your Lordship's Ward."

"Good Heavens!" the Marquis exclaimed. "I had forgotten all about her! Now I think of it, the girl was being brought up by one of her relatives."

"That is correct, my Lord, I knew that I could rely on your memory," Mr. Barrett said admiringly. "When Colonel Langley was killed, his sister-in-law, Lady Langley, had the young lady to live with her and sent her to a good school."

"And what has happened since? Why am I involved?" the Marquis asked.

"I think your Lordship must have forgotten, although I did tell you six months ago, that Lady Langley had died."

The Marquis could not remember this, but he did not interrupt and Mr. Barrett went on,

"The notice of it was in the newspapers because Lady Langley left her niece her fortune, which was a quite large one."

The Marquis thought in that case he would not be expected to support his Ward whom he had never seen.

The background to all this was that Colonel Terence Langley had been his Commanding Officer when he was in the Household Brigade.

He was a charming man and a magnificent rider and he had befriended the Marquis as soon as he joined the

Regiment. Because they were both absorbedly interested in horses, they had spent a good deal of time together apart from their Regimental duties.

Colonel Langley had stayed at Oke Castle and the Marquis had stayed in the Colonel's house in the country when he was arranging a Point-to-Point or a Steeplechase.

There had been one occasion, he now recalled, when there was a race on a particularly dangerous course and before they set out the Colonel had said,

"I suggest that all you young men, if you have anything to leave, should make a will just in case anything nasty happens to you."

This advice was a tradition and they had all laughed. Some of them had made ridiculous wills, which they read out aloud.

When they had finished, somebody had asked the Colonel somewhat impertinently,

"What about you, sir? Have you not made your will?"

"Not for a long time," the Colonel admitted.

"Then come on," everybody shouted, "you cannot give orders and not do what is right yourself!"

Good-humouredly and, the Marquis thought later, because they had all had a great deal to drink, the Colonel had written a will in which he distributed his worldly goods.

He had left his house to his wife, his horses to his brother, his polo ponies to an Officer of the Regiment and his pigs and cows to various friends.

Only when he had finished, after bequeathing a number of other items, did the Marquis ask,

"What about your daughter? We have never been allowed to see her, but I believe you have one."

"I am not having all you young bloods turning her head," the Colonel answered. "But now you mention it, Rayburn, I will leave her to you. You are the richest of this bunch and at least, if I am not here, you can give her a ball and make her the belle of the Season."

The others had laughed uproariously at this.

But the Marquis, who had not then come into his title, had replied that, if the Colonel should die that day, the only ball he would be able to pay for would be a football!

Everybody thought this very funny and they were cracking jokes as they mounted their horses for the Steeplechase in which fortunately nobody was killed.

It was just over three years later that Colonel Langley was involved in a fatal carriage accident.

After his death it was discovered he had never made a later will than the one that he had made before that Steeplechase.

His wife was killed with him and the Marquis, as he was now, then found himself the Guardian of the Colonel's daughter.

He had, however, been staying abroad with friends when the Colonel and his wife were buried and Mr. Barrett had duly sent a wreath with the correct message to the funeral.

He had waited until the Marquis returned before he told him of what had occurred.

"Good God!" the Marquis had exclaimed. "What am I to do with a child on my hands? How old is she, by the way?"

"She is fifteen, my Lord, and there is no necessity for you to worry about her. In your absence I was in touch with her aunt, Lady Langley, the Colonel's older sister. She is having Miss Zia to live with her and will arrange for her education."

The Marquis had given a sigh of relief.

"Thank you, Barrett, I might have known I could rely on you."

"Lady Langley is very well off, my Lord, so, although the Colonel was unable to leave his daughter very much money, she will have everything she could possibly need."

The Marquis had never thought about her again.

Now he asked,

"Why has this Priest come to see me?"

"He has brought with him a letter from Miss Zia Langley," Mr. Barrett replied, "and here it is."

He put the letter in front of the Marquis and, because there was something a little odd about the way he spoke, the Marquis remarked,

"I presume you have already read it. What does it say?"

"Miss Langley asks your permission to become a nun!"

"A Nun?" the Marquis exclaimed.

He picked up the letter as he spoke and read it.

"Dear Guardian,
I wish to take the veil in the Convent of the Holy Thorn and I am told that I have to ask your permission

to do so.

I should be grateful if you would allow this for I know that here I shall be able to devote myself to the worship of God.

I remain,

Yours respectfully,

Zia Langley."

The Marquis read the letter and then he said,

"This seems somewhat extraordinary! How old is the girl now?"

"The Priest says that she is just eighteen."

"And you say that she has recently inherited a large fortune from her aunt?"

"Yes, my Lord."

The Marquis looked down again at the letter.

Then he muttered,

"I think I had better see this Priest."

"I thought that was what your Lordship would wish," Mr. Barrett said.

"What did you think of him?" the Marquis enquired.

Mr. Barrett hesitated.

"I may be mistaken, but I have a feeling that he is not a particularly Holy man. Of course your Lordship may think differently."

"Have you any reason apart from your instinct for thinking this?" the Marquis asked.

"He was here before I was down this morning," Mr. Barrett answered, "and, when the servants offered him a cup of coffee, he asked for a brandy! He explained that he had had a long journey from Cornwall, but it seemed odd for a Priest."

"I agree with you," the Marquis said briefly. "Send him in."

He knew as he waited by his desk that Mr. Barrett had a particularly shrewd instinct and seldom made a mistake where the staff in his houses were concerned.

Only a few moments elapsed before the butler opened the door to announce,

"Father Proteus, my Lord."

A man came into the room wearing a cassock.

He looked over forty with just a touch of grey at his temples.

He was a fairly large man, well-built and certainly, the Marquis thought, he did not look as if he denied himself in any way.

He wore a large decorative crucifix on his chest and he moved with a deliberately slow dignity across the room to where the Marquis was sitting.

The Marquis held out his hand saying,

"Good morning, Father, I understand that you wish to see me.

"God bless you, my son," the Priest said and sat down opposite the desk in the chair that the Marquis indicated.

"This is a very great pleasure for me, your Lordship," he began. "I have heard about your success on the Racecourse and you must have been very gratified at winning so many of the Classics."

"I am indeed," the Marquis answered. "You are interested in racing?"

"I try in a very limited way to be aware of what goes on in the world outside," the Priest replied, "and, of course, Zia Langley has spoken of what a fine horseman her father was."

"He was indeed," the Marquis agreed. "It is very sad that he should die when he was a comparatively young man."

"Very sad indeed," the Priest said, "but he is undoubtedly in Heaven and all he will worry about is that his daughter should be looked after and protected."

"Protected from what?" the Marquis asked bluntly.

"The wiles and wickedness of this dreadful world. Frankly, my Lord, Zia wishes to take the veil and I can promise you that we will look after her and keep her happy until she joins her father in Heaven."

"And you need my approval for this?" the Marquis asked.

It seemed to him that there was a slight change of tone in the Priest's voice as he said,

"If your Lordship would just sign these papers, then I will trouble you no further."

As the Priest spoke, he put two papers down on the table, one, the Marquis saw, gave his permission as Guardian for Zia Langley to take the veil.

The other paper was a form that instructed a Bank to transfer money they held in her name to the Convent of the Holy Thorn.

The Marquis stared at the second paper.

Then he asked Father Proteus,

"Is this transference of money necessary?"

"Those who dedicate themselves to God give up their personal possessions," the Priest pointed out.

"I know that this, where Miss Langley is concerned, will be quite a considerable sum of money," the Marquis remarked.

"It does not matter to us, when a woman wishes to take the veil, if there is very little or a great deal," the Priest responded pompously. "Everything is dedicated to helping the poor and needy and there are, as your Lordship well knows, a great many of those at this present time."

"The poor and needy who will benefit are in Cornwall?" the Marquis asked him.

He had a distinct feeling that the Priest was somewhat surprised by the question, but he answered,

"There are some naturally within our jurisdiction, but we also contribute to the work of our Brothers and Sisters in London and in other great towns where there is suffering and in many cases starvation."

"I suppose I should have asked you this question before," the Marquis said, "but I gather that yours is a Roman Catholic Convent, while Colonel Langley was, as I do know for a fact, a Protestant."

"No, my Lord, you are mistaken," the Priest said. "We are a Teaching Convent for pupils who come to us for tuition not only in the Scriptures but in other subjects as well."

He paused and then went on,

"I persuaded Lady Langley to send Zia to us because we have the best teachers in music and art and she is very interested in both. She came first to us as a day girl."

His voiced deepened dramatically as he continued,

"When her Ladyship went to God, she voluntarily entered the Convent as a boarder and she has been so happy with us that she has no wish ever to leave us."

"It sounds very interesting," the Marquis said, "and, of course, it is something that I would like to see for myself and also to make the acquaintance of my Ward."

Watching the Priest closely, the Marquis was sure that he stiffened before he replied,

"That is quite unnecessary, my Lord, and I would not wish to impose on your Lordship's good nature by asking you to make such a long journey."

He stopped to cough before he continued.

"As Zia says in her letter, she is anxious to take the veil immediately and we shall have a special Service within a week or so when she can do so."

He learnt forward to say even more insistently,

"All your Lordship has to do is to sign these two papers and I will not trouble you any further."

"It is really no trouble," the Marquis said lightly. "I was intending in any case to leave London and instead of going to my Castle, as I had decided to do, I will come to Cornwall. I see from the address that your Convent is not far from Falmouth."

The Priest was silent and before he could speak the Marquis went on,

"I will travel in my yacht and I should be able to call on you the day after tomorrow. Shall we say at twelve o'clock?"

"This is all really quite unnecessary, my Lord," the Priest protested. "I am quite sure that your Lordship will find such a long journey irksome just to see a young girl who will be at her prayers."

"Then I will wait until she has finished them!" the Marquis countered firmly.

He rose to his feet as he spoke and very reluctantly the Priest rose too.

"I am sure," the Marquis said genially, "you would, Father, like some refreshment before you leave. Perhaps a light meal? It is, I know, difficult to find good food on the trains."

He held out his hand as he spoke.

The Priest hesitated and then reluctantly, almost as if he was forced to do so, he shook the Marquis's hand.

"I wish I could persuade your Lordship not to waste your time," he then commented.

"I cannot believe it will be a waste of time," the Marquis asserted, "and I think you will understand that I would not wish to be remiss in anything that might concern the Colonel's daughter."

There was nothing that the Priest could then do but move towards the door and, as the Marquis rang the bell by his side, the butler opened it.

"Goodbye, Father. I will see you on Thursday," the Marquis called after him.

If the Priest murmured anything in reply, he did not hear it.

He waited until a few minutes later Mr. Barrett, as if he knew that he would be required, came back into the room.

"You were quite right, Barrett," the Marquis said, "there is something wrong here."

He held out the two papers that the Priest had given to him as he spoke.

Mr. Barrett read them and said,

"I think, my Lord, that I should get in touch with the Head Office of this Bank and make enquiries as to exactly how much is deposited there in Miss Langley's name."

"That is just what I expected you to say and I am suspicious, very suspicious, Barrett, about the whole set-up. Find out as well who the Convent of the Holy Thorn is affiliated to."

He paused and then continued,

"I doubt if either the Archbishop of Canterbury or the Cardinal of Westminster Cathedral have any connections with it."

"I will find out everything I can," Mr. Barrett affirmed. "In fact, my Lord, I have already heard somewhat strange stories about this particular place."

"You have?" the Marquis asked. "You did not mention anything before."

"I did not wish you to be prejudiced before you had seen the Priest," Mr. Barrett said, "and I have really nothing specific to relate except that one of my relations lives in a village not far from the Convent."

"This might be useful. What does he say about it, Barrett?"

"I saw him about a year ago and I just happened to mention Colonel Langley, whom he admired as he had sold him several horses for the Regiment."

"Go on," the Marquis prompted him.

"He had met the Colonel's daughter, Zia, and he also knew that her aunt, Lady Langley, who sent her to the Convent as a day girl."

"That is what the Priest told me," the Marquis remarked.

"My relative said that he thought it was a strange set-up. There are several nuns, most of whom have been there a long time, and the school which is more or less separate from the Convent."

The Marquis was listening intently as Mr. Barrett went on,

"They managed to collect a number of elderly teachers who had settled in that part of Cornwall."

Mr. Barrett paused and then resumed,

"This naturally resulted, my Lord, in quite a number of the County families sending their daughters there for special lessons, music in particular and art for another."

The Marquis nodded.

"The Priest," Mr. Barrett went on, "and there are a number of them who run the place, are not accepted by the local Clergy. It is only hearsay, but a great amount of alcoholic drink passes through the Convent gates."

Mr. Barrett's eyes twinkled as he added,

"There is always, according to my relative, enough money to pay the farmers for the best young lambs, chickens, eggs and cream and this locally is considered strange fare for those who profess to be fasting a great deal of the time."

"I get the picture," the Marquis laughed, "and that is why I am going to Cornwall!"

Mr. Barrett looked at him in surprise.

"You are really going yourself, my Lord?"

"Most certainly! Let the Captain of *The Unicorn* know that I shall be boarding her this afternoon and I have informed my visitor that I shall be with him the day after tomorrow."

Mr. Barrett laughed.

"You always do the unexpected, my Lord, and your father had the greatest respect for Colonel Langley."

"So had I," the Marquis nodded.

He did not say anything more, but began to sort through his letters.

There was a smile on Mr. Barrett's lips as he sat down on a chair next to the desk and opened his pad ready to take notes of the Marquis's instructions.

CHAPTER TWO

The Marquis joined his yacht immediately after luncheon.

Before he left he wrote explanatory letters to the Prince of Wales and to his hostess for that evening as well as to several others who he had engagements with for the next two or three days.

He was not certain exactly what he intended to do after he had visited the Convent, but he was determined not to come in contact in any way with Yasmin.

Nor did he intend, if Lord Caton died, to attend his funeral.

He knew it was inevitable that there would be some comment about his behaviour.

The question was now where should he go?

He was, however, intent on finding out first about the Convent of the Holy Thorn.

He remembered hearing in the past that women were welcomed in Convents if they had a fortune to endow the Community with.

At the same time mostly this happened in the case of Roman Catholics, who had been educated in a Convent School since childhood.

Alternatively women who had had an unfortunate love affair that had made them feel that no other man could ever fill the place of the one they had lost would dedicate their lives to God.

At least he told himself as *The Unicorn* sailed out of Folkestone Harbour that this was something new for him to do and would help him to forget Yasmin.

Because the weather was warm and sunny and the sea comparatively calm he was glad to be in his splendid yacht.

He had not been in *The Unicorn* for some time, but he always insisted that it should be ready to leave at a moment's notice.

This was in fact a subtle way of keeping his crew on their toes and now he appreciated the advantage of such an order.

Everything appeared to be spick and span and the Captain Blackburn was delighted to welcome him aboard.

"We were hoping that you were coming to try out the new engine we have just installed on the yacht, my Lord," he commented.

"I have not had any opportunity until now," he replied, "but I wish to be at Falmouth by tomorrow night or at least by Thursday morning."

"There's no difficulty about that, my Lord," the Captain said confidently.

He proceeded to show the Marquis how fast *The Unicorn* could move through the water with the new engine and he was on the bridge for most of the afternoon.

In a way he regretted that he had not invited Harry to come along with him.

Then he thought that he did not want anybody in London to know why he had left so precipitately and it would make too good a story to reveal that he was visiting a nun.

He had left a note for Harry, saying that he had to visit Colonel Langley's daughter who was his Ward.

"*I will not be away for more than two or three days,*" he wrote, "*but she has been left a fortune and I am obliged to sort things out.*"

He told Harry to continue to arrange the house party at Oke Castle that would take place the weekend after next.

He knew that Harry would be curious, but there would be plenty of time to tell him the truth if it was necessary after he returned and then swear him to secrecy.

As the yacht moved down the coast, he was aware that he was escaping from a trap that Yasmin had set for him, but he was not yet entirely free.

If she insisted on claiming that she was expecting his baby and took a number of her friends into her confidence, it would undoubtedly be very uncomfortable, to say the least of it, for him to prove otherwise.

Now he thought it over he realised, as he had never done before, that Yasmin had an iron determination when it came to getting her own way.

She had certainly handled him in a subtle manner that had made him think that he was doing the chasing.

When he looked back, however, he realised that it was always Yasmin who had arranged their meetings and planned each time before he left her when they would next be together.

Because he had been infatuated by her beauty, he had been content knowing that to make love to her was what he really wanted himself.

Now he thought, and it was something that he had often thought before, that he disliked being the hunted rather than the hunter.

It was extraordinary how women managed to get their claws into him almost before he knew their names.

As he had a very forceful personality, this did seem rather strange.

He was honest enough to admit, however, that he had a weakness that contradicted the rest of his character when it came to beautiful women, who could always twist him round their little fingers.

'I am damned if I will ever let this happen to me again!' he swore.

But then he had to admit to himself that women were as essential in his life as were his horses.

When he went to his cabin after an excellent dinner provided by one of the chefs who he employed at Oke House, he slept peacefully.

He had chosen the furnishings of his yacht with great care, remembering how he had often disliked the discomfort of the beds in other people's yachts and houses.

He had taken great care to choose mattresses on which, his friends told him, it was like 'floating on a cloud'.

Certainly he did not notice the turbulence of the sea, which was due to a wind that blew from the South. And there was only a slight swell that was not in the least disagreeable.

They sighted the coast of Cornwall late in the afternoon and were actually moving into Falmouth Harbour by dusk.

The Marquis congratulated the Captain on his speed, ate an excellent dinner and retired to bed early.

He made his plans and sent Winton the Mate, who was an intelligent man and had been in the Royal Navy, ashore to find a livery stable.

The Marquis had instructed him to hire the most up to date chaise that was available and the very best horses.

By the time he was having his breakfast, he was informed that, although the chaise was slightly old-fashioned, it was well-sprung and the horses were young and comparatively well-bred.

"That is very good!" the Marquis approved. "And they tell me, Winton, that you are a good shot."

"That was when I was in the Navy, my Lord," the Mate replied, "but I've not used a rifle or a pistol for some years."

"I think it is a skill that you are not likely to forget and I want you to come with me today and carry a pistol with you."

He rose as he spoke from the table in the Saloon and went to a drawer in a piece of furniture that was fitted to the wall of the cabin.

He then unlocked the drawer. There were three pistols in it and the Marquis took one out and handed it to Winton.

"I will tell you why this may be necessary on our way to where we are going," he said, "and we leave at eleven o'clock."

"Very good, my Lord."

The Marquis liked the way the man responded to his instructions without asking any questions.

He knew a great deal about all the men he employed on *The Unicorn* and he was aware that Winton was spoken of as being very accurate with a rifle.

He had also at one time boasted that with a pistol he could hit a playing card thrown into the air through the centre of it.

As the Marquis then drove away from the quay, he found that the horses were exactly as Winton had described.

He therefore settled down to enjoy his drive to the Convent, which Mr. Barrett had told him was about five miles inland from Falmouth.

The countryside they passed through was very beautiful with small green fields and tall hedges.

Although the Marquis had never visited Cornwall before, he could well understand why Cornish people extolled their County.

He remembered that he had two friends with estates here that they were volubly devoted to.

Then he knew that Winton was waiting to hear what lay ahead and he said, choosing his words carefully,

"I may be wrong, Winton, but I rather suspect that a fraud is taking place at a Convent that we are going to now. While I am inside the building, I want you to use your eyes and see if you think that there is anything suspicious going on and, of course, to listen attentively to anything anybody says to you."

He looked at Winton to see if he was paying attention and went on,

"I also wish to leave quickly if it is necessary. If by any chance, which is very unlikely, anybody tries to prevent me from doing so, be ready to fire your pistol not at the person in question, but over his head to frighten him."

"I quite understand, my Lord," Winton replied.

The Marquis noted with amusement that there was a note of excitement in his voice that had not been there before.

He knew that like all young men, he was looking forward to what might be a skirmish or, if not, certainly an adventure.

It was just a few minutes before noon when the Marquis, having followed Mr. Barrett's instructions and the signposts, saw the walls that he guessed must enclose the house and the grounds of what had once been a private residence.

He saw that he was not mistaken as he drew up at two big wrought-iron gates and saw that they were surmounted by a Coat of Arms that he was sure must have belonged to a noble family at one time.

A gatekeeper came from a lodge and opened the gates and as he did so the Marquis noted that he used a key to unlock them.

He drove in, but stopped beside the gatekeeper to ask,

"Am I right in thinking that this is the Convent of the Holy Thorn?"

"That be right, my Lord," the man replied with a broad accent. "They tells I you were expected."

"Thank you."

The Marquis drove on and found that the house was only a short distance in front of him.

It was an attractive building with a gabled roof and was surrounded by a garden that was bright with flowers while the lawns were well tended.

The Marquis brought his horses to a standstill at an imposing front door that again had the same Coat of Arms in stone on the portico.

He handed his reins to Winton and stepped down from the chaise as the door opened and a man stood there wearing a monk's robe.

He then bowed awkwardly and the Marquis thought that he was a rather surly-looking individual with a pugnacious chin and heavy body.

He would have looked more at home in a boxing ring than in a Chapel.

"I have called here to see Father Proteus," the Marquis began, "as I expect you already know."

"Please come this way," the man suggested, walking ahead heavily in shoes that seemed unnecessarily coarse in contrast to his robe.

He showed the Marquis into a large sitting room overlooking the garden.

He was surprised at the damask-covered sofa and chairs and there were several pictures on the walls that he reckoned were valuable.

He only had the time, however, to have a quick look round before the door opened and Father Proteus came hurrying in.

"Welcome, my Lord," he greeted him affably. "It is delightful to see you. I hope you had a smooth voyage."

"I enjoyed it," the Marquis replied, "and I hope that you too did not find your journey from London too arduous."

Father Proteus held up his hands.

"The train is quicker, although not and never will be as comfortable as a carriage."

"I agree with you," the Marquis smiled.

The door opened and the servant who had admitted him to the Convent came in with a tray on which there was a bottle of wine and two glasses.

He set it down on a table and Father Proteus said,

"I feel sure, my Lord, that you are in need of a little refreshment. It is a warm day and the dust on roads always makes one thirsty."

The Marquis accepted a glass of wine, aware as he did so that it was an expensive vintage that he sometimes bought himself.

He took a few sips and then suggested,

"As I am sure, Father, you are very busy, I would like to see Zia Langley immediately."

"Yes, yes, of course," Father Proteus replied. "She will tell your Lordship how contented she is with us here in this happy House of God surrounded by the beauty of nature."

He spoke in a somewhat theatrical manner and the Marquis made no reply.

Father Proteus left the room to return almost at once, so that she must have been waiting outside, with a young woman.

She was dressed in black and wore a dark veil over her head that the Marquis knew was that of a Postulant.

She came towards him, her head bowed, and dropped him a curtsey after which she straightened herself to face him.

As he looked at her, the Marquis was shocked.

Zia Langley was undoubtedly a very plain young woman, in fact he doubted if he had ever seen or at least noticed such a plain girl before.

She had a thin face, a large nose and the suspicion of what the doctors called a 'harelip'.

It struck him that the poor girl was almost repulsive.

She did not look young, but she might have been any age.

Then, as he looked into her eyes, which were brown, he saw, again to his surprise, that she was afraid.

"It is a pleasure to meet you, Zia," he said holding out his hand.

"It was kind of you to come and see me," Zia replied in a low voice, which again the Marquis was aware held a note of fear in it.

"I was very fond of your father," he replied, "and I can only regret that we have not met before."

"I miss Papa very much."

As she spoke, the Marquis was thinking of how good-looking the Colonel had been. In fact he was often teased about it in the Regiment by the other men.

They would say that, when he was in his uniform and on parade, he looked exactly the handsome Cavalryman the public expected.

"When you are there," a Subaltern said once to him, "the girls cheer as we ride down The Mall, but they don't give us a glance!"

How was it possible, the Marquis wondered, that such a good-looking man should have produced such a plain daughter?

Then he remembered admiring Mrs. Langley when he had been staying at their house and thinking that she was very attractive.

She had blue eyes and fair hair.

And almost as if the words were put into his mouth, he asked her,

"I have always wanted to know what happened to Joker."

As he asked the question of her, he saw a blank expression come into Zia's face and instinctively she looked towards the door that had been left ajar when she entered the room.

The Marquis was sure then that, while Father Proteus had not come in with her, he was listening to their conversation outside.

Almost as if it was a cue for his entry, the Father appeared in the doorway.

"I was wondering, my Lord," he said, "if you would like Zia to show you the Chapel where she prays and where, when you have given your consent, she will take the veil."

"How kind of you," the Marquis replied, "but I have a better idea. I would like to talk to Zia alone and, as it is such a warm day, I think we should go into the garden and enjoy the sunshine."

Father Proteus frowned and the Marquis realised that he wanted to refuse his suggestion.

There was a French window in the room and he walked towards it.

Without waiting for Father Proteus's permission, he opened it and stepped out onto the terrace outside.

As he did so, he was almost certain, although he could not have sworn it in a Court of Law, that Father Proteus took hold of Zia's arm, saying as he did so almost beneath his breath,

"Be very careful what you say."

There were three steps down onto the green lawn and, when Zia joined him, the Marquis walked away from the house towards the flowerbeds bright with flowers.

"This is a charming garden," he remarked conversationally but rather louder so that his voice would carry, "I am sure you enjoy being in it."

"Yes, my Lord."

The Marquis walked even further away from the house, at the same time admiring the flowers that were in the shadow of some trees.

He knew that they were being watched by Father Proteus from the window and he walked on still further with Zia beside him.

Her head was bent as if she was too shy to look at him.

When he was certain that they were completely out of earshot and it would be difficult for Father Proteus to see them unless he moved to another window, the Marquis urged her,

"Don't be afraid. I promise I will not hurt you in any way."

The girl beside him looked up and now her eyes were wide with what he recognised was fear.

"I want your help," the Marquis said, "and I need it badly! As I am sure you are a good girl, I am pleading with you to tell me the truth."

"I-I don't – understand."

"I think you do," the Marquis said. "Where is Zia? Why is she not allowed to see me?"

The girl then drew in her breath and would have looked wildly back at the house if the Marquis had not put his arm round her shoulders in what might have been an affectionate gesture.

"Trust me," he persisted, "and, as I have already asked, help me."

"How did you know that I was – not Zia?" the girl whispered.

"Because you are not in the least like her father or her mother."

"They – they chose me because I am so – ugly they thought you would think there was nothing strange in my wanting – to take the veil."

"I guessed that," the Marquis replied, "but where is Zia?"

"Locked in her room – until you have gone."

The Marquis could see a wooden seat just ahead of them under some trees and he led the girl to it and sat down.

As she sat down too, he took her hand and slipped it through his arm.

"Now look as if we are having a happy confidential talk about your childhood and your life here."

"They will kill me if they think – I have betrayed them," the girl said miserably.

"What is your name?" the Marquis asked.

"Sister Martha."

"And what is your position in the Convent?"

"I am a nun as I have been for two years now and I have very little to do with the pupils who come here for tuition."

"But you know why they want to keep Zia?" the Marquis asked.

Sister Martha nodded her head.

"She is very rich – and they are always wanting – more money!"

"Who are 'they'?"

"Father Proteus and there are four other men – who run the Community."

"Are they really Priests?"

"I don't know. Father Anthony, an old man who was here before they came, is very ill and his sister was the Mother Superior – who looked after the nuns like myself."

"And what has happened to her now?"

"She died and Father Anthony – does not know what is going on."

"What *is* happening here?" the Marquis asked.

"I don't really know," Sister Martha replied, "but there was another girl who was rich like Zia and – she was forced to become a nun because they – wanted her money."

"What happened to her?" the Marquis enquired.

The Sister looked away from him.

"Tell me!"

"I am – afraid!"

"They cannot overhear you now," the Marquis pointed out.

There was silence and then in a voice that he could hardly hear Sister Martha stated,

"She – she tried to escape and I think – they killed her."

The Marquis drew in his breath.

And then he said,

"You have to help me, Sister, and if you do so, I promise you, when Zia gets away from here, I will have this whole place investigated."

"They will surely – kill me," Sister Martha shook with fear, "if they think I have told you – anything!"

"They will not know that you have said anything that has made me suspicious if you will do exactly as I say."

"I am – so afraid," she murmured. "I know that what is happening is wrong and wicked, but I have nowhere else to go and nobody wants me – because I am so ugly."

"Listen to me, Martha," the Marquis urged her in a quiet voice.

She turned her face to look up at him and he said,

"I promise you that, if you will help me to get Zia away from here, I will see that you are provided for for the rest of your life. If you want to go into another Convent, that shall be arranged for you. If you want to be free, I will find somewhere for you to live with people you can be happy with."

He saw that the Sister look at him as if she could not believe what he was saying.

He smiled at her in a way that women find irresistible before he went on,

"Just trust me and help me now as no one else can."

He felt the Sister's fingers tighten on his arm as she replied,

"I will try, but I know that Father Proteus – is watching us."

"Then what we have to do," the Marquis said, "is to convince him that I believe you are Zia and that I am prepared to sign the documents he has prepared for me, which state that I am quite happy to leave Zia Langley here."

He saw that Sister Martha was looking at him in a bewildered fashion and he went on,

"As soon as Zia is released, will you tell her that I have come to rescue her?"

"But how?" Sister Martha asked. "How can you – do it?"

The Marquis thought for a moment.

Then he looked through the trees to where he could see the walls that surrounded the whole Convent.

"Don't turn your head," he said, "just tell me if there is any place where Zia could climb over this wall."

"There is one place – at the end of the garden where there is an oak tree – that Zia can climb."

She was speaking very softly and after a moment she went on,

"Once she climbed the tree to look out and Father Proteus saw her and was very angry! She was punished by being put on – bread and water for three days."

The Marquis's lips tightened, but he did not say anything.

"Will she be allowed into the garden after I have gone?" he asked after a moment.

"We are allowed to walk on the lawn within sight of the windows – twice a day," Sister Martha said.

"And what is the last time you do so?"

"At four o'clock before we have our tea and after that we are locked in – for the night."

"Very well," the Marquis said, "at four o'clock tell Zia when she is in the garden to get as near to the tree as possible, then make a sudden dash, climb it and I will be waiting for her on the other side of the wall."

"It will be – difficult," Martha answered him unhappily.

"If it is and she is prevented from escaping, tell her that I will come to the Convent this evening and take her away by force!"

Martha could not prevent a little cry from escaping her lips.

"Be careful!" she warned. "The servants Father Proteus employs are – very strong and, since Zia is being forced into becoming a nun, they patrol the grounds to make certain that she cannot escape."

She saw the Marquis square his chin and those who know him, as Harry did, would have been aware that he was very angry.

Then he said,

"You are very brave, Sister, and I admire you very much. Now, when we walk back I want you to look happy as if I have agreed to everything you have asked of me and, when I have said 'goodbye', I know that Father Proteus will be pleased with you."

"Who is the 'Joker' you spoke about?" Martha enquired.

"He was a magnificent stallion that Zia's father always rode and won a great number of hair-raising Steeplechases on."

"They did not tell me that."

"And if you had been able to answer that question plausibly, I had several others," the Marquis smiled.

He rose to his feet, but kept Sister Martha's arm through his.

"We are going back now, "he said, "as I don't want Father Proteus to be in the least suspicious. When I leave, they will think that I am returning to my yacht, but make quite certain that Zia is aware that I am waiting for her."

"Once you have gone – I am sure they will release her."

When he was certain which was the oak tree at the end of the garden that Zia must climb, the Marquis walked with Sister Martha slowly back towards the French window that they had left the sitting room through.

As they came within earshot of Father Proteus, he said in a clear voice,

"I remember your father taking a six foot jump and making us all follow him. We would have looked very foolish if we had failed when a much older man had succeeded."

As he spoke, the Sister was looking up at him as if she was thrilled by every word he said.

"Your mother was also a good rider," the Marquis went on as they reached the steps up into the sitting room, "at least so I have been told, although actually I never saw her on a horse."

He climbed the steps and, seeing Father Proteus in front of him, exclaimed,

"I have been talking to Zia about the old days. I suppose, Father, that the pupils in the Convent are not allowed to ride?"

"It can be arranged if it is something they are eager to do," Father Proteus replied. "In fact I have often thought that amongst the other subjects in the curriculum, riding should be included."

"It is certainly the best exercise in the world," the Marquis informed him. "But then I am prejudiced."

"Of course," Father Proteus answered. "And your Lordship has the finest horses."

They went into the sitting room and the Marquis said to Sister Martha,

"Goodbye, my dear, it has been delightful meeting you and I entirely understand why you wish to spend the rest of your life in this lovely place."

He had taken her hand in his and Sister Martha replied in a breathless voice,

"Thank you, my Lord. Thank you very very much."

She curtseyed and then, as if she was shy, she went from the room leaving the Marquis alone with Father Proteus.

"A charming girl," the Marquis said. "It is sad when her father was so handsome that she should be so plain."

"I felt that your Lordship would understand why she would be happier with us than in the outside world," Father Proteus replied.

"Of course," the Marquis agreed, "and it is probably the right solution. At the same time it is a great pity, and in a way very unfair, that some women should be so beautiful and others extremely ugly."

"We can only believe, my Lord, that God knows best and there are compensations, as for Zia, in finding the beauty of their souls."

The Marquis sighed and then said,

"I must go back to my yacht. I have, as I am sure you will understand, a great number of engagements in London."

"I am certain that you have, my Lord, and it was very generous of you to spend so much time on poor little Zia."

The Marquis moved towards the door.

"One moment, my Lord," Father Proteus said hastily. "I think you have forgotten that we need your signature on the form of consent for Zia to take the veil."

"So you do!" the Marquis exclaimed. "How stupid of me. I have left the papers in my yacht."

"I am sure that I can provide you with duplicates," Father Proteus suggested.

"There is no need to trouble yourself," the Marquis replied. "I will sign them before I leave Falmouth and hand them over to the Harbourmaster. You will be able to collect them tomorrow morning."

"Yes, of course, my Lord," Father Proteus agreed, "but it will take only a few minutes for me to find you the duplicates."

The Marquis drew out his gold watch.

"You must forgive me, Father, but I have someone waiting for me and I am late already."

He had reached the front door almost before Father Proteus realised what was happening.

Shaking the Priest hurriedly by the hand he reached his hired chaise and sprang into the driving seat.

"Goodbye, Father," he called out, raising his hat.

"God go with you, my son," the Father answered.

His words were lost in the whirl of the Marquis's wheels and the crack of his whip.

He was down the drive and out of the gates, which had been left open for him, before Father Proteus moved.

With a smile of satisfaction on his face he walked back through the open door.

*

The Marquis waited until they were some distance away from the Convent before he asked,

"Did you notice anything strange while I was inside the Convent, Winton?"

"Nothin' much, my Lord," Winton replied, "except there was several men lookin' out of different windows. Seemed a bit odd in a Convent that I thinks was for women!"

"That was observant of you," the Marquis replied. "Now, what we are going to do, Winton, is to kidnap a young lady who is being held prisoner there, get her to the yacht and out to sea before the men you saw looking out of the windows can stop us!"

"How are we goin' to do that, my Lord?"

"It will not be easy. They may want to make quite certain that we have left, so look back and see if by any chance we are being followed."

Winton did as he was told, finding it difficult to peer through the cloud of dust that the horses and the chaise raised on the dry road.

After straining his eyes for some minutes he reported,

"There be no one in sight, my Lord."

"Then look out for the first Posting inn we come to where we can have something to eat," the Marquis proposed, "and then we will return!"

He could tell that Winton was excited, but he said nothing, only looking ahead of him.

Suddenly Winton called out,

"There it be, my Lord! That's the main highway, which I notices when we was comin' here. There must be an inn of some sort where the stagecoaches stop."

"You are quite right, Winton," the Marquis agreed, "and, if there is one, we will find it."

About twenty minutes' drive further on they came to an attractive little inn called *The Cock and Hen*.

It was obvious that the landlord was very impressed by the Marquis and, while he could not offer him an elaborate meal, what was obtainable was certainly edible.

The Marquis was wise enough not to sample the wine, but enjoyed the homemade cider from Devon.

When he had finished and was no longer feeling hungry, he called for the landlord and then asked him,

"Tell me about the Convent you have near here."

"A strange place, zir, to be sure," the innkeeper replied. "They do say that the lasses the gentry sends there be well taught, but the Priest who runs it be an odd cove!"

"Is he a Cornish man?"

"Not as I understand it, zir, and they as be with 'im are not the sort I likes to see in my bar!"

The innkeeper then obviously did not wish to say anything more and, picking up the bill, the Marquis settled it including a generous tip.

The innkeeper bowed respectfully as he said,

"Thank you, sir, thank you! I 'opes I might 'ave the pleasure of servin' you again!"

The Marquis thought that it was unlikely, but he did not say so.

He then went out of the dining room, where they were the only guests, to see that the innkeeper had retreated behind the bar.

He asked him if he had a map of the neighbourhood.

"I doubts there be one, zir," he replied, "but I can tell you anythin' you wishes to know."

"Well, suppose," the Marquis said, "I take the Convent of the Holy Thorn as a centre point which we both know. What I wish to do is to travel behind it as if I was going North, then turn and approach it from that direction rather than the way I have just come."

It took a little time to explain to the innkeeper exactly what he wanted.

He was then told that there was a lane that would take him about half-a-mile North of the Convent so that, when he approached it from there, he would be facing South.

This was exactly what the Marquis required and, following the innkeeper's directions, he and Winton set off.

By this time it was after three o'clock and they only had a short way to go before they saw the Convent ahead of them.

The Marquis realised that there was no entrance apart from the gates in the South wall that he had passed through earlier.

At exactly four o'clock he drew up on the narrow road below the ancient oak that Sister Martha had told him Zia could climb.

He told Winton to change his seat from the one beside him to the one behind which was intended for a groom.

Then, looking up at the boughs of the tree, he found himself praying that Sister Martha had been able to tell Zia that he was waiting and that she would be able, unless Father Proteus was suspicious, to reach the oak tree.

He listened and he thought, although it might have been his imagination, that he could hear voices in the garden.

Then suddenly there was a rustle amongst the leaves overhead and the next moment he saw the face of a girl peering over the wall.

It was then he said to Winton,

"Quickly! Catch her!"

Putting his pistol down on the seat, Winton jumped down from the chaise and went to the wall.

The girl flung her legs over the wall and holding tightly to the top of it, she lowered her body with a swiftness that told the Marquis that she was athletic as her father had been.

Then, as she hovered above his head, Winton grasped her ankles.

Suddenly there were shouts and then a shrill scream from the garden.

"Quickly!" the Marquis ordered.

A second later Zia sprang into the chaise beside him and the horses were already moving as Winton jumped up behind.

"They – saw me!" she gasped.

"I heard them," the Marquis said grimly. "Hold on tight! The quicker we get away from here the better."

He cracked his whip and the horses surged forward.

There was a long expanse of the wall to pass before they came to the South entrance of the Convent.

Just before they reached it, Father Proteus ran into the centre of the road waving his arms and behind him were four other men running through the gate.

The Marquis did not slow his speed.

He drove his horses straight at Father Proteus and only at the last moment when the Priest realised what was intended did he try to move out of the way.

But it was too late.

The wheel caught him and there was a scream as he fell to the ground and a bump as it passed over his leg.

As it did so, Winton fired his pistol twice over the heads of the men who were reaching out to grab at the chaise as it passed them.

They instinctively ducked and as they did so the Marquis, driving at even greater speed, enveloped them in a cloud of dust.

He drove on for some distance before an excited voice beside him stammered,

"You have – saved – me! *You have – saved me*! Just how can – you have been – so wonderful?"

CHAPTER THREE

The Marquis, intent on his horses, did not turn his head until they had travelled some way.

Then, when he realised that they were now quite a distance from the Convent, he looked round at Zia.

He saw two very large, dark blue eyes in an exquisite little face that he thought was outstandingly pretty.

Then he decided that the right word was '*lovely*'.

She was, he thought, exactly what he would have expected the Colonel's daughter to be like and he then said with a smile,

"Now I know that you really are your father's daughter!"

Zia laughed.

"It was very clever of you to guess that Sister Martha was – impersonating me."

"Not really," the Marquis answered. "I could not believe that your father, who was one of the most handsome men I have ever met, could have produced anything so plain."

"You saved me!" Zia enthused. "I cannot think of how to thank you, my Lord."

"We will talk about that later," the Marquis replied. "For the moment the quicker we can get away from here the better."

They drove for some way in silence before Zia said,

"Sister Martha told me that you had promised to look after her and Father Proteus will certainly punish her. If he throws her out of the Convent, she has nowhere else to go."

"We must rescue her as quickly as possible," the Marquis said, "and you must tell me, Zia, how you managed to get yourself in such a mess."

There was silence between them and, since he thought that perhaps it was embarrassing, he suggested swiftly,

"Keep it until I have you safely on board my yacht."

Zia gave a little cry of excitement.

"You came in your yacht?"

"I thought that perhaps Father Proteus might have told you."

"He told me nothing! When I was locked in my bedroom I guessed that something was happening, but there was no way that I could escape."

As the road was twisting and narrow at this point, the Marquis had to drive carefully in case they should encounter another vehicle coming in the opposite direction.

He did not therefore ask the question that he was most curious to know the answer to.

Only when they drove down to the Falmouth quay and he saw *The Unicorn* looking very large and white ahead did he think with a sense of relief that they were now out of danger.

A seaman was waiting to run to the horses' heads and the Marquis, putting down his reins, alighted and then went round the chaise to help Zia to the ground.

But, without any assistance, she sprang out with the swiftness of a young fawn.

Now he could look at her properly, he saw that she was, as he had already ascertained, very beautiful indeed.

At the same time she looked somewhat strange with her long gold hair flecked with red falling over her shoulders.

She was wearing a hideous black dress made of a coarse material and, when she started to walk towards the gangway, he realised that she did so in her stockinged feet.

He knew without being told that she had been given a pair of the thick-soled ugly shoes that were worn by nuns and she had kicked them off so as to be able to climb the tree more easily.

As the Marquis reached the deck where the Captain was waiting, he gave him his orders,

"Put to sea at once, Captain Blackburn, with all possible speed and make for Plymouth."

"Very good, my Lord."

The Marquis followed Zia into the Saloon and, as she heard the engines starting beneath her, she clasped her hands together and cried,

"I cannot believe – this is – true! I thought I was – doomed and the – only way I could escape would be by – dying!"

The Marquis replied quietly,

"It's all over now and I think we should celebrate by having a glass of champagne."

"That is – what Papa used to do when he – won a Steeplechase!"

The Marquis gave the order for the champagne and by the time it arrived the yacht was out of the Harbour and into the open sea.

Zia was watching through the porthole and, as the yacht began to feel the pressure of the waves, she sighed as if she was speaking to herself,

"Now I am – no longer – afraid."

"Come and sit down," the Marquis suggested. "Drink a little of your champagne and tell me exactly what has happened to you."

Zia obeyed him and he thought that, despite the irregular movement of the yacht, she had an unmistakable grace in the way she walked.

"I was a day girl at the Convent while my Aunt Mary was alive," she began, "and when she died – Father Proteus suggested that I came to stay as a boarder for a – little while until I could find – a relative or somebody else to – chaperone me."

"Why did you not write to me?" the Marquis asked.

"Had I done so before I went to the Convent, you might have received my letter. I wrote several times after I arrived there until I became aware that there was no hope of your ever receiving them."

The Marquis frowned.

"That man who calls himself 'Father Proteus' must have planned it from the moment he heard that you were your aunt's heir."

"I realised that – afterwards," Zia said in a low voice, "and, of course – after the funeral, when the Solicitor told me how – rich I was, everybody was – talking about it."

The Marquis was about to comment, but she cried,

"If you only know how I have gone over it, night after night and thought how I should have been in touch with you or some other relatives, before I – listened to – Father Proteus."

"I quite understand that it seemed the easiest thing to do at the time," the Marquis said.

"I was so upset at losing Aunt Mary and also Cornwall was a long way from the people I had known when Papa and Mama were alive, but it was – stupid of me – very stupid."

"Stop blaming yourself," the Marquis replied. "You could hardly have guessed that the man who called himself a Priest was nothing more or less than a criminal."

"When he told me I had to – take the veil," Zia went on, "I thought he – must have gone mad! Then I was moved into the nuns' part of the house well away from the pupils who came every day for their lessons, many of whom were – my friends. It was then I – realised that I was – his prisoner."

"It must have been very frightening," the Marquis remarked sympathetically.

"I was – terrified!" Zia admitted. "I had no idea that the men Father Proteus employed, who only came in for a few hours every day, were thugs who would knock anyone out or ill-treat – an intruder."

Zia paused to cough and then resumed her story,

"If they had caught – us just now when they came – through the gates – they would most undoubtedly have knocked you unconscious – if they had not – killed you!"

"I can hardly believe it," the Marquis exclaimed. "It seems incredible to me that these evil characters have not been discovered before now."

"Sister Martha said that she had told you about – the other heiress whom they – most certainly killed once they had their – greedy hands on her – money."

"Did nobody investigate her death at the time or make enquiries?" the Marquis asked.

"They said that she had fallen down a flight of stairs and – broken her neck, "Zia replied. "Which in fact was – what she had – done except that they had – pushed her."

There was a little tremor in her voice that told the Marquis it was what she had expected might happen to her.

"It's all over now," he repeated comfortingly.

She did not reply and after a moment he asked,

"What are you thinking?"

"It passed through my mind that Father Proteus will not give up – so easily," Zia said in a low voice. "Also – if you intend to report to – anybody what has – happened, then I am sure that he will – try to avenge himself in some way or another."

"I think that is highly unlikely. What I have to do, Zia, and I know you will understand, is to speak to the Lord Lieutenant of Cornwall and also to the Chief Constable."

Zia did not reply and after a moment he went on,

"Apart from anything else we have to save Sister Martha. I promised that I would look after her in the future and find her somewhere to live if she does not wish to go into another Convent."

"She is a very good person," Zia said, "and I think she would be happiest in a Convent, but not – like the one that we have just – left!"

She shuddered and, because the Marquis thought that it was a mistake to let her go on worrying, he said,

"I imagine that the first thing we have to do now is to find you something to wear."

Zia laughed.

"I had forgotten how extraordinary I must look! When they moved me into the nuns' side of the house, they gave me what I am wearing now and took away all my own clothes."

"I daresay we can find you something in Plymouth," the Marquis commented, "that will save you from arriving in London looking like a crow and after that Bond Street will be at your disposal!"

Zia looked at him and then she asked,

"My – my money is – safe?"

"No one can touch it without my permission," the Marquis replied, "and I will notify the Bank where you are as soon as we arrive at my house in Park Lane."

Zia smiled before she said,

"Thank you! Thank you, my Lord, for thinking of – everything. I can hardly believe that I no longer – need feel so afraid or expect to be – killed once Father Proteus has taken – possession of – everything I own!"

"If we can prove that he definitely killed that other girl who was an heiress," the Marquis said thoughtfully, "or conspired with others as an accessory in murdering her, then he will undoubtedly be hanged."

He knew by the expression on Zia's face that only then would she feel that she was completely free Father Proteus

He told himself that it was inevitable, having suffered so much at the man's hands, that the whole experience would upset her for a long time.

But he was certain that once she was in a different environment and was enjoying the Social Season in London as she should be doing at her age, it would soon fade from her mind.

Because he thought that it was important, he deliberately talked to her about the old days.

He told her how fond he and all his brother Officers had been of her father and praised his brilliant riding.

"I suppose you ride yourself?" he asked her.

"I had horses when I was living with Aunt Mary," Zia replied, "but it was not the same as riding with Papa. He always inspired me to do better."

"That is what I think we all felt when we served under him," the Marquis reflected.

It was dark before the yacht reached Plymouth.

The Marquis had written two letters, which he arranged for one of his seamen to deliver immediately.

One was to the Lord Lieutenant of Cornwall and the other to the Chief Constable of the County.

He thought that it would assuage any nervousness Zia might feel at being still not a very great distance from Father Proteus.

He therefore ordered Winton and another member of his crew to be on guard all night, both of them armed.

*

The following morning, as soon as the shops were open, Captain Blackburn went ashore.

His instructions were to buy some clothes for Zia that would at least make her look more conventional than she did at the moment.

She had dined with the Marquis the previous night wearing his silk nightshirt and a robe that he wore in the summer and was therefore made of a thin material.

Because it was much too long, she had turned up the hem and the cuffs with safety pins.

There was a sash to tie round her small waist and it seemed in some strange way quite a becoming garment.

Being a deep sea blue it echoed the colour of her eyes, which the Marquis thought were different from the blue of any other eyes he had ever seen.

He had never actually dined alone with a young girl before.

He had always imagined, when his relatives kept telling him that he must take one for a wife that she would undoubtedly be not only boring but ignorant of anything that he himself was interested in.

Zia, however, looking very young, talked to him of horses that she knew a great deal about.

She also knew the history of her father's Regiment and that of several others that the Marquis was interested in and was extremely knowledgeable about them.

She asked him intelligent questions about his estate and, because she had always lived in the country, they could discuss rural problems.

These included persuading the labourers to accept new machinery, the innovation of which they were extremely suspicious.

In fact by late evening the Marquis thought that he might have been dining with Harry for they would have discussed very much the same subjects.

He sent Zia to bed early, knowing that she was tired not only from the drama and anxiety of what had happened during the day, but he understood from what she had said that she had not slept properly for a long time being so afraid of what might happen to her in the future.

He could hardly believe it possible that Father Proteus would have actually dared to murder her.

Yet what was to stop him once he had complete control of her money?

When the Marquis himself eventually went to bed in his comfortable cabin, he was still thinking over what had happened during the day and all that he had heard.

It was difficult to believe that he had not stepped into a drama that was taking place in a Playhouse.

Or he might have been reading a horror novel where everything that happened sprang from the frightful imagination of the author who had written it.

It never struck him when he did fall asleep that he had not given one thought to Yasmin since the previous evening.

*

The Marquis had finished his breakfast and was wondering if Zia had eaten hers in her cabin when she came into the Saloon.

For a moment he just stared at her.

Then he realised that, if last night she had seemed attractive in his robe with her hair tied back with a piece of ribbon, now dressed as a young lady she was breathtaking!

The best that Plymouth could provide was a simple summer gown of some thin material. The skirt was full with a fairly small bustle at the back while Zia's tiny waist was encircled by a blue sash that almost matched her eyes.

The Captain must have bought her hairpins a well for she had arranged her hair in a chignon.

The Marquis noticed that she had a long swan-like neck besides an exquisitely curved figure.

She stood for a moment in the doorway of the Saloon and, as he rose to his feet, he said,

"You look now exactly as your father would have wanted you to!"

Zia laughed delightedly.

"I feel more like myself again and I have already thrown that hideous nun's robe out of the porthole."

The Marquis laughed.

"I hope it sank to the bottom taking all your worries with it!"

Zia sat down at the table and the Stewards brought in the dishes that had been kept hot until she appeared.

"I forgot last night," she said as she helped herself, "to thank you for the first delicious meal I have had for months. I so enjoyed talking to you that I forgot my manners."

The way she spoke, the Marquis thought, was quite different from the way any other woman would have expressed her pleasure of his company.

Whereas last night he had thought, as he looked at Zia, that she was little more than a child, today she was a young woman, one he was aware would appear like a shining light in London Society.

He had already planned while he was dressing that he would ask his grandmother if she would present Zia to the Social world.

The Dowager Marchioness, although she was now getting on for seventy, was still very active.

She found the pretty Dower House at Oke Castle boring because she was so often alone. So she made every possible excuse to go to London and she stayed at the Marquis's house in Park Lane, where she had once been the most celebrated hostess in the Social world.

'Grandmama will enjoy having a *debutante* to look after,' the Marquis mused, 'and, as Zia is so entrancing, it will not be at all difficult to find her a suitable husband.'

It struck him that, as she was so rich, there would inevitably be a multitude of fortune-Hunters who would pursue her.

He told himself severely that, as her Guardian, he must be careful to ensure that she was married for herself and not for her money.

Now, looking at her, he was quite certain that there would be dozens of men who would fall in love with her almost as soon as they saw her.

He knew that, if he was to be a conscientious Guardian for his Ward, it would take up a great deal of his time.

He was not sure if he resented that prospect or whether it might provide him with a new interest.

"Are we going to stay here long?" Zia asked as she put down her knife and fork.

It was a simple question.

But the Marquis was aware that she was still frightened that Father Proteus might appear in some devilish way of his own and drag her back into his clutches.

"We will leave the moment I have spoken to the Lord Lieutenant," he replied, "but I am afraid, Zia, you will have to answer a certain number of questions about the Convent."

He thought that she was going to refuse and he added quickly,

"I know it is uncomfortable for you, but we must think of Sister Martha and also make quite certain that these criminals do not force other helpless girls into their clutches, who are not as agile as you are at climbing oak trees."

He spoke lightly to relieve the tension and Zia answered him,

"Of course I must and perhaps the old nuns will be able to stay on, even though I am sure that Father Proteus has either spent or crooked away every penny that was there before he arrived."

The Marquis learnt next morning that the Convent had at first been for older women who had nowhere else to go.

Then it had been more or less appropriated by Father Proteus, who realised rapidly that he was on to a good thing.

His friends had moved in and, because the old Priest was too ill to argue with them and the Mother Superior was very frail, they had simply taken possession of the house. And there had been no one with enough standing or determination to prevent them from doing so.

"After that had happened," the Chief Constable related, who had arrived at the same time as the Lord Lieutenant, "your Lordship will understand that unless somebody complained, there was no reason for me to interfere with what on the surface appeared to be a pious Religious Institution."

"I do understand that," the Marquis replied, "but now something has to be done about it."

"Of course it must," the Lord Lieutenant agreed.

He was a distinguished Peer whom the Marquis had met before at Windsor Castle.

When he learnt what had occurred, he insisted that they should take immediate steps against Father Proteus.

The Chief Constable took a long statement from Zia and she gave him useful information about the Convent and the way it was run.

Then, because the Marquis was in a hurry to get away, both the Lord Lieutenant and the Chief Constable promised that, when they had investigated further, they would send a report to the Marquis in London.

"You will understand that I shall be very curious," the Marquis said. "At the same time I should be grateful if you would try to ensure that my Ward's name is not brought into any public statements."

He looked at the Lord Lieutenant as he spoke who answered at once,

"I understand your concern, Okehampton, and I will do all that I can to prevent anything appearing in the newspapers."

The Marquis thanked him and, as soon as the two gentlemen had left, he told the Captain to put to sea immediately.

"The whole problem is now out of our hands," he said to Zia, "and so we can relax and enjoy ourselves."

"It is very kind of you to be so concerned about – Sister Martha."

The Marquis had said that, if Sister Martha was in any distress, the Chief Constable was to arrange for her to travel to London and she could stay at Oke House until her future was settled.

"I will, of course, pay all the expenses," the Marquis added, "and also the expenses of somebody to travel with her so that she will not be alone on the train."

Now he turned to Zia,

"We must always remember that, if Sister Martha had not been brave enough to allay Father Proteus's suspicions, you would not be here now."

"I will give her anything she wants," Zia said positively. "She is really my responsibility, my Lord, not yours!"

"We will not quarrel over her," the Marquis smiled, "and I think we will both see that Sister Martha is very much happier in the future than she has been in the past."

"If only we could only change her face, the poor thing," Zia said. "She always talks of herself as being ugly and I know it worries her."

"I expect, unless she wants to go on being a nun, pretty gowns and her hair arranged in a more attractive fashion would make all the difference," the Marquis remarked.

"We could certainly try," Zia answered, "and it will be like having a handicapped child to look after."

They both laughed at the idea.

Then to speak of a child made the Marquis remember Yasmin and her assertion that he had given her a baby.

Once again the anger he had felt at being deceived and threatened by her swept over him.

As it did so, Zia exclaimed,

"W-what have I – said wrong? What has – upset you?"

She sounded so worried that the Marquis replied quickly,

"It has nothing to do with you just something I remembered that has made me angry."

Then, as still she looked at him with worried eyes, he asked her,

"How can you be aware of what I am thinking? I have often congratulated myself on being perceptive, but it is not something I expected to find in you, Zia."

"I think it is something I have – always had," Zia answered, "in fact I could often read Papa's thoughts before he had put them into words. Mama told me that it is because we have Celtic blood in our veins."

"As your Guardian," the Marquis said with mock seriousness, "I forbid you to read my thoughts! They are often not suitable for a well-bred young lady to know about."

Zia laughed.

"Now you are making me curious, my Lord, and I shall try harder than ever to find out exactly what you are thinking."

"Am I to believe that you are defying me?" the Marquis enquired. "In which case I shall take a very strict line in seeing that you obey my orders!"

Zia laughed again.

"If I am too young to be perceptive, you are certainly too young to be a Guardian! They are usually old with grey hair and come in the same category as grandfathers!"

"That is how you should think of me," the Marquis commented.

She gave him a mischievous smile that he thought was particularly attractive before she replied,

"Now you are trying to frighten me and, as I refuse, now I am free, to be frightened any more, you will have to think of a better way to keep me in order."

He found that, as the day progressed, Zia seemed carefree for the first time.

She teased him and had what he could only describe as a *joie de vivre* that made them both laugh a great deal.

The hours seemed to pass more quickly than he could have imagined possible.

*

He had decided that they would stay the night in a quiet harbour and reach Folkestone early the following morning when they would take the train to London.

Then he realised that he was enjoying himself more than he had thought possible and had no desire to go back to London too quickly.

He therefore told his Captain to sail on round the coast and move up the Thames as he had often done before to disembark at Westminster.

"I am glad that is what you have decided to do," Zia said when he told her. "I love being at sea and it is so delightful to be with you, my Lord, because you make me think – of Papa."

The Marquis thought with a twist of his lips that, when he was with most women, he did not in any way remind them of their fathers.

Despite the fact that Zia was laughing with him as if he was a contemporary, he was aware that she did not think of him, as any other woman would have done, as an attractive man.

He supposed it was because she was so young and, as he had already found, completely innocent of the world.

The strange thing was that while there were none of the *double entendres* that were so much part of the conversations he had with the beauties who he and Harry pursued, he found her interesting and intelligent.

When he thought about it, he had to admit that he had not been bored for one moment since they had been together.

He knew that, when Yasmin or any of his previous loves had been alone with him in the yacht, every word they spoke was flirtatious and every look of their eyes would hold an invitation.

It would have been impossible for him to be with them for any length of time without holding them in his arms, kissing them and eventually taking them below to his cabin.

But it clearly had never entered Zia's mind that she should try to attract him as a woman.

When they went to their separate cabins before dinner, the Marquis changed first and was waiting in the Saloon for Zia to appear.

The yacht was anchored in a small bay where there was shelter from the wind as well as any rough movement of the sea.

The Stewards had not yet turned on the lights in the Saloon, but there were candles on the table, which made the dinner laid for two seem very romantic.

The Marquis always looked particularly magnificent in evening clothes and, as he waited for Zia, he gazed out through the porthole knowing that the stars would soon begin to twinkle overhead.

It was a warm evening and he thought that any other woman who was with him would be waiting for the moment when they would both go out onto the deck that would be flooded by starlight.

She would look up at him and her long neck and profile silhouetted against the darkness would be alluring and very seductive.

Every movement would be an invitation for him to put his arms around her. Then his lips would hold her captive and he would kiss her until they were both breathless.

He then became aware of the sound of light footsteps coming up the companionway and a second later Zia was in the Saloon.

"Look at me in my finery!" she exclaimed.

She spread out her arms sideways as she spoke and twirled round so that the Marquis could see the movement of her full skirt and the little cascading frill running round the hem.

Her shoulders were bare and her waist seemed to be even smaller than it had during the daytime.

Her gown was of a very pale green, the colour of the early buds in the spring.

With the candlelight picking out the red in her hair, she looked, the Marquis thought, like a sprite who must have come from the waves.

There was something ethereal about her and at the same time it was as if she moved to music.

"I must certainly congratulate the Captain," the Marquis said. "His taste is impeccable!"

"That is what I thought," Zia agreed, "and I must now show him how smart I look."

She did not wait for the Marquis to reply, but went out of the Saloon and onto the deck. Then he heard her running forward towards the bridge.

He could not help smiling as he followed her.

He was thinking that none of the beauties who he and Harry had found so alluring would think that the Captain's opinion of their appearance of any importance.

On the other hand they would undoubtedly expect a eulogy from him.

'I must not spoil her,' the Marquis told himself as he reached the bridge.

"I am glad you are pleased, Miss Langley," he heard the Captain say. "In fact my wife always asks my advice before she buys a new gown."

"Then you can tell her that his Lordship thinks your taste is impeccable," Zia answered, "and I think really you ought to come and advise me when I reach Bond Street!"

The Captain laughed.

"I'm a much better judge of ships than I am of gowns, Miss Langley, and this is one of the finest ships I've ever handled."

"Now *I* am receiving the compliments!" the Marquis remarked as he joined them.

"And quite rightly," Zia enthused. "*The Unicorn* is magnificent!"

As they moved back towards the Saloon, the Marquis could not help wondering whether she thought that the owner of it was magnificent too.

He was so used to compliments from any woman he was interested in that he now found, although he admitted it was ridiculous, that he missed them when they were not there.

When they sat down to dinner, Zia found the food as excellent as it had been the night before and quickly forgot about her appearance as once again they were talking of the old days.

"Perhaps I shall not be – with you," she said a little wistfully, "but if I am – and you hold a Steeplechase – would you allow me to ride in it?"

"Certainly not!" the Marquis asserted. "Steeplechases are not for women, but, if I do arrange a Point-to-Point, which I usually do sometime in the summer, then I will introduce a 'Ladies' Race' that you can compete in."

Zia regarded him quizzically for a moment before she said,

"As Papa's daughter, if you will lend me one of your Lordship's superb horses, I would much rather race you."

"And you really think you might win?" the Marquis asked.

He expected her to say that was impossible, but she would like to try.

Instead after a moment she replied,

"I think I might have a sporting chance if you allowed me to choose the horse I would want to ride and – then to get to know it well before the race."

The Marquis raised his eyebrows and she explained,

"Papa said that, while horses love racing, it is always right to talk to them about what is happening and also, if they are used to their rider, they know what he expects of them and will want to please him."

The Marquis wanted to say that she was just being imaginative.

Then he remembered how the Colonel had said very much the same thing to his young Subalterns before they competed in the many Regimental races when the Household Brigade always distinguished themselves.

"What I am saying," Zia went on, "is that if I can talk to my horse and let him know that he is to beat yours, perhaps we shall pass the Winning Post – ahead of you."

"I think you are using magic," the Marquis said, "and that is distinctly a contravention of all the rules of the game!"

Zia merely chuckled.

"If I have the chance to show you what I mean," she said, "you will understand."

The Marquis, as it happened, did understand.

He had never before met a woman who knew the secrets that were used by the gypsies and by the jockeys, who were most successful in the races that they rode in.

When it was time to go to bed, he admitted that he had enjoyed himself a great deal and was also more certain than ever that Zia would be a great success in London.

'She is original, she is unusual and very lovely!' he murmured to himself.

He decided that he would tell his grandmother that he would give a ball for her at Oke House in London and another one at Oke Castle.

'No girl could ask for more,' he told himself, 'and by the time she is dressed better than any other *debutante*, she will quickly capture some distinguished young aristocrat and I shall have done my duty nobly as her father and mother would expect me to do.'

Then, as he attempted to think who amongst the young men he knew would be the most suitable as Zia's husband, he found himself discarding first one and then another.

They might be 'blue-blooded', they might have distinguished names and important titles to inherit.

But, when he thought them over, they did not seem to qualify for anybody as unusual or as lovely and ethereal as Zia.

He knew that with her large fortune, she could most certainly pick and choose.

But it was unthinkable to imagine her married for instance to a certain young Peer of his acquaintance who did nothing but pursue actresses and pretty 'Cyprians' as he had done ever since he had left his school.

Two other young Noblemen were, to the Marquis's certain knowledge, keeping 'Pretty Horse-Breakers' in smart Villas in St. John's Wood.

From the conversations that he had had with Zia, he knew that she had no knowledge of what were called 'other interests' in a man's life.

And she would undoubtedly be extremely shocked when she learned about them.

There was something very pure and innocent in her large blue eyes.

As the same time they held a certain mystery that the Marquis was aware was something spiritual and not what was usually associated with the word where it concerned a woman.

'*Damn it all!*' he exclaimed to himself. 'There must be some decent man about, a man who would be faithful to a wife if she was like Zia.'

Then he found himself wondering if in the future she would become like Yasmin and all the other beauties who had given him their favours over the years.

He knew that, when he had dined in another man's house in his absence, eaten his food and drunk his finest wines and then enjoyed himself with his wife, he had always felt slightly ashamed.

To him it was almost like picking someone's pocket.

Yet it was all part of the Social world that he moved in.

He more or less accepted it that, if a husband did not look after his wife or had 'other interests', there was no reason why she should remain faithful to him.

And yet, he told himself firmly, it was what he would expect of his own wife.

Then, he thought cynically, that he was asking too much.

How could he be sure if he was away from home for even one night that his wife would not have a lover creeping up his stairs and into his bed?

Because he felt almost tormented by the idea, he threw off the bedclothes and went to one of the portholes in his cabin.

He pulled back the curtains and saw the stars filling the great arc of the sky with their light reflected in the sea below them.

It was very beautiful and very romantic.

The Marquis gazed out of the porthole for a long time and then went back to bed saying violently to himself beneath his breath,

'All women are unfaithful, treacherous and deceitful! I will never marry!"

CHAPTER FOUR

The Unicorn reached London and anchored alongside the Embankment above London Bridge.

Thanks to the Marquis's usual efficient arrangements, his carriage drawn by two horses was waiting for them and he took Zia ashore.

She thanked the Captain very prettily for the voyage, saying how much she had enjoyed herself.

When they drove off, she said with a lilt in her voice,

"This is very – very – exciting!"

"I hope you will enjoy yourself in London," the Marquis said, "and I want to show you my Castle in Sussex as well."

She smiled at him.

"And, of course, my Lord, I am longing to see your horses."

The Marquis was wondering if he should include her in the party that he was giving next weekend.

As Yasmin would not be present, there would be an empty place, but he then realised that it was not the type of party that he should take a *debutante* to.

'I will leave her in London with my grandmother,' he decided, 'and she can come to The Castle the week after.'

When they arrived at Oke House in Park Lane, he could see that Zia was impressed by the majesty of the mansion and, when she entered, by the furniture and pictures.

He was, as it happened, exceedingly proud of the house, which had been redecorated by his mother who he always considered had excellent taste.

There was none of the clutter of aspidistras, antimacassars and the knick-knacks that had become fashionable since Queen Victoria had come to the Throne.

The Dowager Marchioness had been brought up in a Regency House and she admired that period more than any other, thinking it more suitable for her husband than the fashions that had recently come into vogue.

Zia was not aware that she was seeing what the Victorians thought was old-fashioned and out of date.

She only knew that it was stunningly beautiful and appealed to her in a way that was difficult to express.

The Dowager Marchioness had been informed of her grandson's imminent arrival and was waiting for them in the drawing room that extended over the whole of the first floor.

It was a classically delightful room hung with pictures that were mostly French and lit by huge chandeliers with a hundred tapers in each one.

It looked to Zia just like a Fairy Palace.

The Marquis noted and was surprised that Zia was not in the least shy at meeting his grandmother, who overawed most people she came into contact with.

She curtseyed to the Dowager gracefully and then said eagerly,

"I have been longing to meet you, ma'am, after all his Lordship has told me about your parties that were the most original ever given in London."

The Dowager Marchioness laughed.

"Is that what you expect me to give for you?"

"Oh, no!" Zia answered. "But I was thinking – as I came into the room how lovely you must have looked against a background that is almost a scene from a Shakespearean play."

The Dowager Marchioness laughed again.

"I think, Rayburn," she said to her grandson, "Zia is thinking of us as idealised figures from Ancient Greece instead of real and often tiresome people."

"I am certain that does not apply to you, Grandmama!" he said. "At the moment I am delighted to be taken as an idealistic figure rather than a disillusioned human!"

He saw his grandmother give him an enquiring glance and he was aware that he had spoken bitterly without thinking.

He therefore quickly told her of how he had rescued Zia from Father Proteus and added when she had listened to him in astonishment,

"It is a story that you must keep to yourself for, as you well know, Grandmama, it could very easily be the talk of every drawing room and every Club in London."

"I have never heard of anything so disgraceful," the Dowager Marchioness said. "You poor child! You must have gone through agonies before my grandson so brilliantly rescued you."

"It was very – very frightening," Zia related, "but his Lordship has told me to forget it – and that is what I am – trying to do."

"You will forget it as soon as we have bought you the prettiest gowns we can find and my grandson has sent out invitations for your ball."

She looked at the Marquis with a questioning look in her eyes and he responded,

"I intend to give a ball here, Grandmama, and also one at The Castle. It is what I know Zia's father and mother would want me to do."

"Of course they would," the Dowager Marchioness approved. "And, because you want Zia to be asked to everybody else's balls, you must send out the invitations as quickly as possible."

"I am dreaming that this is happening!" Zia said. "It's so exciting that I want to dance and sing and make quite sure that I don't wake up!"

The Marquis and his grandmother laughed.

Then when they went down to luncheon, the Marquis could feel her enthusiasm infecting him and he thought perhaps that it might be quite amusing to give a ball at Oke House, which he had never done before.

After luncheon the Dowager Marchioness ordered a carriage and announced that she was taking Zia shopping.

"We will choose from gowns that are immediately obtainable," she said, "and have them sent here for you to try on. We will also order a great number to be made as fast as possible and then buy the accessories to go with them."

"It sounds a phenomenal task," the Marquis observed. "I am glad you don't want me to accompany you."

"I can imagine nothing we want less!" his grandmother replied. "Like all Englishmen you would sit looking bored and thinking that to be inside on such a sunny day was a crime against nature."

Zia laughed.

"Of course he would. Papa always said that he enjoyed seeing Mama looking beautiful in a new gown, but he had no wish to hear about it before she was actually inside it!"

The Marquis accompanied them to the front door to see them off in the carriage.

Then he went into his study where he guessed that Mr. Barrett would have a huge pile of letters waiting for him.

He was not mistaken and, as Mr. Barrett joined him, he said,

"There are two letters, my Lord, which I thought you would wish to see first. One from the Bank giving you a detailed account of Miss Langley's fortune and the other from the Lord Lieutenant of Cornwall."

"I was hoping that I would hear from him," the Marquis exclaimed.

Mr. Barrett handed him the letter and, as the Marquis read it, his expression changed.

"You have read this, Barrett?" he asked.

"Yes, my Lord."

"How could that damned man have got away so quickly? How could he have been aware that the Chief Constable intended to arrest him?"

"Bad news travels on the wind, my Lord," Mr. Barrett remarked.

"I can only suppose what happened was that he had somehow learned that *The Unicorn* had docked at Plymouth Harbour and drew the conclusion that I was communicating with the Lord Lieutenant and the Chief Constable."

"I am sure it must have been something like that," Mr. Barrett agreed, "and, as you see, the Lord Lieutenant reports that there is no one left in the Convent except for the nuns and the old Priest who is too ill to know what is going on."

The Marquis glanced down at the letter again.

"He writes that he has arranged for Sister Martha to leave for London today so we shall know more when she arrives this evening."

"As it will be very late, my Lord," Mr. Barrett suggested, "would it not be best for the young woman to go straight to bed and let you have a talk with her in the morning?"

"I will do so," the Marquis said. "At the same time it does worry me, Barrett, that that criminal gang are still at large."

"Does your Lordship think," Mr. Barrett asked hesitatingly, "that Miss Langley is in any danger from them now?"

"One never knows. Naturally they will be extremely resentful that she escaped and that we are fully aware of their appalling plan to seize her fortune."

Mr. Barrett looked concerned.

Then the Marquis said, as if he was reassuring himself,

"It would be a great mistake to upset Miss Zia by alarming her and actually I cannot believe that this man, Proteus, which I suspect is not his real name, would be so stupid as to attract attention to himself when he knows that the Police are already looking for him."

"I am sure you are right, my Lord," Mr. Barrett agreed, "and anyway now that Miss Zia is under the chaperonage of her Ladyship, she will not be going anywhere alone."

"No, of course not," the Marquis nodded.

Equally he thought that he would make it clear to his grandmother that Zia was not to go to any place where Proteus might be lurking.

He would certainly see when they went to the country that the footman on the box of the carriage always had a loaded pistol in a pocket specially designed for one.

It was something that had been very necessary in the days when highwaymen were to be found in many parts of the country especially in the South.

It was some years now since the Marquis had heard of an incident of that sort and he was sure that most people left their pistols at home or, if they were in the carriage, they were not loaded.

But he now assured himself that he was being needlessly apprehensive in thinking that Proteus would risk his freedom, if not his life, in doing anything so outrageous.

Aloud he said,

"I will have a word with Miss Zia and we certainly do *not* want the servants talking about it or the coachmen looking out for trouble."

"No, of course not, my Lord."

Mr. Barrett then handed the Marquis the letter from the Bank.

It consisted of several pages of figures detailing deposits and shares.

When the Marquis looked at the last page where the total had been calculated, he was astounded.

He had gathered from what Mr. Barrett had said that Lady Langley had left Zia a large fortune, but it was very much bigger than he had anticipated.

Mr. Barrett was aware of his surprise and, before the Marquis could say anything more, he explained,

"When her Ladyship married the Colonel's brother, she was not, I gather, very rich, but over the years a number of her relatives died and bequeathed to her a great deal of what they owned. Apart from that her money has been so well invested that it was in some instances her investments have increased one hundred fold."

"I understand," the Marquis said. "At the same time it is not always a good thing for a young girl to own so much."

"I am sure that your Lordship is thinking of the fortune-hunters," Mr. Barrett remarked.

"I am and I look to you, Barrett, to keep a strict watch on the young men who knock on the door, send flowers and *billets-doux* to Miss Zia, so that we can nip them in the bud."

"I think you will find," Mr. Barrett said, "there is hardly a man in London who would not be eager to get his hands on such an enormous fortune apart from the fact that Miss Langley is one of the loveliest young ladies I have ever seen."

"I cannot think why I always get myself into this sort of mess," the Marquis remarked irritably. "You know as well as I do, Barrett, that if she marries the wrong type of man, I shall have it on my conscience for the rest of my life."

Mr. Barrett was obviously thinking of an appropriate reply when the door opened and Harry Blessington came into the study.

"Hello, Rayburn," he called out to the Marquis. "Thank goodness you are back. I have missed you."

"I am back," the Marquis replied, "and I have a job for you."

"A job?" Harry queried.

The Marquis handed him the letter that he had received from the Bank.

As he did so, Mr. Barrett slipped away, knowing that the two close friends would have a great deal to say to each other.

Harry read the letter that the Marquis handed to him and then gave a long low whistle.

"I thought you would be surprised!" the Marquis stated.

"Surprised? I am astounded!" Harry answered him. "Who could have guessed that the Colonel's daughter would turn out to be 'Miss Croesus'?"

"It's a pity that the Colonel himself could not have enjoyed some of it himself," the Marquis commented. "He would have had even better horses than he owned already!"

"Tell me what she is like?" Harry asked. "If she is not a good rider, I will never believe in heredity again."

"I have a great deal to tell you," the Marquis said.

As he spoke, he sat down in a comfortable chair and, when Harry sat beside him, he told him exactly what had happened when he had arrived in Cornwall.

Harry listened intently without speaking until he had finished and then he said,

"Good God, Rayburn! If I did not know you so well, I would think that you had been drinking! It's all the theatricals I have ever watched at the Playhouse rolled into one!"

"That is what I thought myself," the Marquis replied. "The question is what are we going to do about it?"

"You mean the story is not finished?"

"Not while that fake Priest and his cohorts are still at large. And that is where you have to help me."

Harry glanced at the Marquis.

And then he said,

"Of course I will. This will give you something new to think about, which I feel is rather important at the moment."

"What do you mean by that?" the Marquis enquired.

"I have some bad news for you."

The Marquis stiffened.

He knew perceptively before Harry said anything more what the news would be.

"I have just heard," Harry began, "that Lord Caton died last night!"

It was what the Marquis had feared, but had expected to hear.

But he knew at once from the tone of Harry's voice that there was more to it.

He waited and Harry went on,

"You will not like this, but my friend, Irene, who is coming to The Castle this weekend, received a letter from Yasmin Caton only yesterday."

The Marquis waited, knowing before Harry spoke what was in the letter.

"Yasmin told Irene, of course in complete confidence, that you had asked her to marry you as soon as she was free and that she was carrying your child!"

It was what the Marquis knew he would be told and yet to hear it spoken out loud hit him like a blow.

He rose to his feet to stand with his back to Harry looking down at the fireplace, which, because it was summer, was filled with flowers.

"It's a lie!" he thundered after some minutes of silence.

"I know that," Harry replied. "But what are you going to do about it?"

The Marquis turned round.

"What the devil can I do?" he asked.

*

Coming back from Bond Street, Zia thought that it had been thrilling to see the latest and most elaborate fashions available in London.

The Marchioness had chosen a large number of gowns to be delivered to Oke House for her to try on.

After being forced to wear the hideous black gown that she had thrown into the sea and beneath it the coarse cotton underclothes that were correct for a nun, she had revelled in the silk nightgowns and négligées in the shop that specialised in such intimacies.

"It is all so delightful!" she cried as they drove back to Park Lane. "And how can I thank you, ma'am, for being so kind to me?"

"I am enjoying myself just as much as you are," the Dowager Marchioness replied. "I suppose that every woman dreams of the moment when she can buy the most expensive and the most beautiful clothes of the day and having a large Bank Account to pay for them!"

Zia was still for a moment and then she said slowly,

"You must help me, ma'am, to spend a great deal of my money on other people who are in need of it."

The Marchioness looked at her tenderly before she answered,

"Of course I will help you, my dear."

"I am sure that his Lordship will be able to advise me as well," Zia went on, "because I have no wish to find that anything I give for those who are starving or ill-treated has been put into the pocket of somebody like Father Proteus."

The Dowager smiled.

"You are very sensible, child, and that is exactly what you need to be. Money is always a responsibility and I am glad that you want to help others not as fortunate as yourself."

"Of course I do," Zia replied, "and I would like, if his Lordship will allow me, to send somebody who is competent and kindly to look after the old nuns left behind at the Convent."

She sighed before she continued,

"They often went short of food while I am sure that Father Proteus was stuffing himself with the best fare in another part of the house."

"We will talk to my grandson about it," the Dowager Marchioness suggested.

"I am only hoping," Zia said reflectively, "that Father Proteus and those horrible men who were with him are now behind bars."

It was a question that she asked the Marquis after dinner when his grandmother had gone upstairs to bed and Harry, who had dined with them, was out of the room.

They had talked about everything else of interest at dinner except for Zia's experiences in Cornwall.

Yet she was intelligent enough to realise that the Marquis was keeping something from her.

Now, when he came back into the drawing room, having seen his grandmother up the stairs, she said,

"I know that you must have heard from the Lord Lieutenant and the Chief Constable by now. What have they done with Father Proteus?"

The Marquis wanted to lie to her, but then thought that it would be a mistake.

As he hesitated, Zia came in quickly,

"He has got away, has he not?"

"Yes," the Marquis admitted reluctantly. "When the Police reached the Convent, there was no sign of him or his men."

Zia clasped her hands together and he saw that fear was back in her eyes.

"H-he will – never forgive me – and perhaps whether he has my money or not – he will want to – kill me."

"Nonsense!" the Marquis stressed to her sharply. "You are not to think such things. He ran away because he was frightened and somebody must have warned him that the Police were coming to arrest him."

He spoke very positively as he went on,

"For all we know he may have taken a ship to America or is hiding in Scotland or the North of England. He knows that there is nothing now he can squeeze out of you."

"But – he might take his – revenge."

"Not if it is not going to pay him to do so," the Marquis said. "Be sensible, Zia, and remember that now you are with me he knows that he has nothing to gain by pursuing you when there are a great many other women in the world who he will be able to extort money from."

"You – are right – of course you – are right!" Zia said. "At the same time – I am – frightened."

She shuddered and added in a small voice,

"I have lived under the same – roof with him and I know – how ruthless he was and how utterly he is always determined at getting his – own way."

"I can only repeat," the Marquis said, "that he will be no danger to you or to me, so let's forget him."

He saw the worried expression was still on Zia's face and added,

"Sister Martha is arriving late this evening and I suggest you concentrate on deciding how to make sure that the poor girl is very much happier in the future than she has been in the past."

"She is coming here?" Zia asked. "I am so glad! Father Proteus has not injured her in any way?"

"Perhaps he is not as dangerous as you think he is," the Marquis reflected.

But he knew by the expression in Zia's blue eyes that she was still afraid and nothing he could say or do would drive away her fears.

*

It was after midnight when Sister Martha was brought by a Courier chosen for her by the Police to Oke House.

On the Marquis's instructions, Mr. Barrett escorted her upstairs to the housekeeper who showed her into a comfortable bedroom.

While a maid unpacked the small suitcase she had brought with her, a meal was brought up on a tray.

Sister Martha enjoyed every mouthful of it and afterwards climbed into bed to sleep peacefully.

When she awoke, which was early because she was used to saying her morning prayers in the Chapel at six o'clock, she looked round the bedroom, which seemed to her very grand.

She was thinking how the old Priest had been too ill to give the Benediction in recent months when the door opened and Zia peeped round it.

When she saw that Sister Martha was awake, she gave a little exclamation of joy and went to her bedside.

"You are here and it is lovely to see you," she said.

Then, as she looked at her more closely, she asked,

"What has happened? How have you bruised your face?"

"Saul hit me!" Sister Martha answered. "You remember him the man with the scar?"

Zia sat down on the bed.

"I always thought he was horrible like the others and I was afraid that one of them might do something like this. Are you all right?"

"He knocked me down and I think I became unconscious," Sister Martha replied. "When later I was able to enquire what had happened, I found that Father Proteus, whose leg was injured, had left the Convent with all the four men, taking with him everything that was valuable."

Zia looked at her wide-eyed as Sister Martha went on in a shocked voice,

"You will hardly believe it, Zia, but Father Proteus took all the things from the Altar, the candlesticks, the Communion vessels and even the Cross because it was made of silver."

"He is the most evil man who ever existed!" Zia exclaimed. "But why did the Police not catch him?"

"They arrived too late," Sister Martha answered. "I heard somebody say that a man had ridden in very late the night you left and what he told Father Proteus made him realise that he must escape while he had the chance."

Zia reckoned that this was what the Marquis thought would have happened, that a spy in Father Proteus's employ had watched as *The Unicorn* put into Falmouth.

So they would have known then that the Marquis was communicating with the Lord Lieutenant and the Police.

"Have you any idea where they might have gone?" Zia asked Sister Martha.

She shook her head.

"He might be anywhere, but I imagine that he will be in London."

"Why London?" Zia asked curiously.

"I heard him say once a long time ago when he did not know I was listening, 'I am fed up with this place! It gives me the creeps! I want to be back amongst the bright lights of London'."

Zia was frightened again.

"I must tell the Marquis what you have told me," she said, "and, Sister Martha, you have to be very careful of yourself. I am sure that Father Proteus would be furious to know that – you are – here."

"He will not worry about me or you," Sister Martha said, "now that he cannot get hold of your money."

"He will certainly not be able to do that now that the Marquis is looking after it."

"If you ask me," Sister Martha said, "he will find some other place that he can take over, just as he took over the Convent, and where he can persuade people in different ways to lend him money."

Zia knew that this was true.

Father Proteus had been able to deceive her aunt into thinking that he was a good and helpful Priest.

And there had been a number of other parents in the County who sent their children to the Convent because

~96~

Father Proteus had promised that they would be well educated.

When she thought about it, she knew that he had been astute enough to employ a really accomplished music Teacher and a painter, who certainly achieved some good results from their pupils.

There were also three elderly and competent Governesses who made a number of other subjects interesting so that the pupils were eager to learn.

Later, when she discussed it with the Marquis, she said,

"When you think of it, my Lord, it was an extremely clever way of doing really nothing except to find out what other people wanted. He had a house to live in and the fees were very high, although I now suspect that he did not pay the Teachers very generously."

"And nobody had any idea he was anything other than what he appeared to be?" the Marquis asked.

"No, of course not. He talked as if he was a genuine and dedicated Priest and after Father Anthony was taken ill he occasionally, if there were any visitors to the Convent, conducted a Service in the Chapel. But now I know that it was sheer blasphemy for which he ought to be struck down by a thunderbolt!"

The Marquis smiled.

"Let's hope that will happen," he said, "but, as we shall never know the truth, let's forget him."

Zia thought that it would be impossible, but she did not say so.

They talked about Sister Martha and the Marquis, with a kindness that Zia thought was unusual in such a consequential man, questioned her as to what she would like to do.

"If you wish to go into another Convent," he said, "I will arrange with the Archbishop of Westminster Cathedral that you are accepted into the best one he can recommend."

Sister Martha drew in her breath, but she did not speak and the Marquis went on,

"There is another idea that you might find interesting. Why not put aside your nun's attire for a while and stay, either here or in the country, and find out if you prefer an ordinary life to one of dedication?"

He knew before he said so that Sister Martha would feel embarrassed at the thought of living with them and he added,

"I have a feeling that you would like to help other people. Now I have a school on my estate in Sussex where the Mistress who has taught in it for many years is growing old."

He saw Sister Martha's eyes light up and he continued,

"Mr. Barrett tells me that she is already looking for her successor. Until she finds one, perhaps to help her out is something that you might contemplate doing. She has room in her small house for any assistant I send her."

Before Sister Martha could reply, Zia exclaimed,

"That is a wonderful idea! And if I come to The Castle, as his Lordship has said I am to do, I will be able to visit you and make sure that you are really happy."

Sister Martha was unable to answer because her eyes had filled with tears and it was impossible for her to speak.

Zia jumped up and put her arms round the older girl saying,

"There is no hurry for you to make up your mind. Just think it over. We will talk about it and then tell his Lordship in a day or two."

"You are – very kind," Sister Martha stammered, "and I don't know – what to say."

Then because Zia was sure that the Marquis would find tears tiresome, she took Sister Martha out of the study where they had been talking.

The Marquis was left alone and he walked to the window to look out into the garden.

He was thinking that few women of his acquaintance would be so kind as Zia was being to the plain little nun who she really she had nothing in common with.

He could never remember any of the beauties who he had spent time with worrying over anyone except themselves.

He had often thought that they were quite unnecessarily sharp and intolerant even to their personal servants.

'Zia has been well taught by her father,' he told himself.

Then he sensed that it was not teaching that made Zia care for others but her warm heart and that was very different.

Now he was alone he was forced once again to remember what Harry had told him and to know that Yasmin was making sure in a very subtle manner that it would be impossible for him to escape her.

Of course Irene would talk, however confidential the secret might be that she had been entrusted with.

The Marquis knew that he was fortunate that where Harry was concerned it would go no further.

Harry had assured him that he had made Irene swear on everything she held Holy that she would not repeat what Yasmin had written to her to another living soul.

But few women were trustworthy he was sure of that.

No one could be certain that Irene would not, naturally in confidence, tell another friend, who would tell another and then yet another.

Within a few days the story would be all over London.

'What shall I do?' the Marquis asked himself a dozen times. 'What *can* I do?'

As he spoke the words beneath his breath, the door opened and Harry came in.

"I am sorry I am late, Rayburn," he said, "but one of my horses has gone lame and I went to the Mews to see to him."

"You can always borrow one of mine," the Marquis offered him.

"That is what I was just going to ask you," Harry replied. "What are you going to do?"

"I was just thinking of going riding, "the Marquis replied. "Then we have a luncheon party today, to which, if you remember, you are invited."

"Of course I remember. If there is one person I enjoy talking to it is your grandmother."

The Marquis stared out of the window as Harry went on,

"By the way I have not had a chance to tell you how much I admire your Ward. She is lovely, Rayburn, quite,

quite lovely! I only hope that you enjoy her looks while you have her with you, because she will not be with you for long."

"For God's sake," the Marquis replied irritably, "don't start harping on about the girl being married before she has even attended her first ball."

"I would not mind betting that by her second she will have had half-a-dozen proposals!" Harry persisted.

The Marquis did not reply and after a moment his friend carried on,

"Do stop, Rayburn, looking like a bear with a sore head. If it is Yasmin who is worrying you, I think I have a solution."

"You have?" the Marquis enquired.

He thought as he spoke that Harry was just being facetious.

Because he had lain awake most of the night worrying as to what he should do, he did not find it a laughing matter.

"It's quite simple," Harry said, "and I cannot think why we did not think of it before."

"Think of what?" the Marquis wanted to know.

"That you should get married!"

CHAPTER FIVE

The Marquis stared at Harry and was about to reply when the door opened and the butler announced,

"Lord Charles Fane, my Lord."   .

A good-looking and impeccably dressed young man came into the room saying as he did so,

"I have just learnt, Rayburn, from your grandmother that you are back in London and I decided to come and see you right away."

The Marquis held out his hand.

"How are you, Charles? Behaving badly as usual, I suppose?"

"Of course," Lord Charles replied, "but I wanted to talk to you for a moment about your party as unfortunately Evelyn's husband has just returned from the North and therefore she cannot come."

"Another casualty!" Harry exclaimed before the Marquis could speak.

"Hello, Harry," Lord Charles greeted him. "Who is the first one?"

Realising that he had made a mistake, Harry replied hastily,

"Rayburn will tell you our troubles."

"Before I do that," the Marquis said, having no intention of confiding in Lord Charles, "would you like something to drink?"

"Naturally," Lord Charles responded. "I always think that your champagne is medically speaking the best tonic I know."

The Marquis laughed and went to the grog tray, while Lord Charles seated himself in a comfortable chair near Harry.

"I was wondering what had happened to you," he said to the Marquis who had his back to him, "when I just happened to meet your grandmother, who was accompanied by the most beautiful creature I could possibly imagine!"

"That is exactly what I have been saying," Harry chimed in.

"She really is unbelievably lovely," Lord Charles went on, "and, if you don't ask me to dinner, I shall sit on your doorstep until I can see her again!"

He was speaking lightly, but the Marquis suddenly felt annoyed.

He knew that Charles Fane was one of the most amusing men in London, but at the same time, he did little but trek from boudoir to boudoir and his love affairs were too numerous to count.

He was the last man he would think of as suitable to be with anyone as innocent as Zia.

"Now listen to me, Charles," he said as he handed him a glass of champagne, "Zia is young and unspoilt. Harry and I are going to find her a suitable husband among the young men who do not have a reputation like yours. So keep away!"

Lord Charles stared at him.

"Are you really giving me orders, Rayburn?" he asked. "I have never heard anything so outrageous and I have no intention of being told to keep off the grass where anything so delectable and unusual is concerned."

The Marquis felt his temper rising.

Then he told himself that if Zia looked on him as a father figure, she would presumably feel the same about Lord Charles, who was two years older than he was.

Equally he would take care that she saw as little of him as possible.

"Now, what I want to know," Lord Charles was saying, "is where you found her and who she is."

As the Marquis did not reply immediately, Harry obliged by saying,

"She is Colonel Langley's daughter. You must remember him."

"Of course I remember him. The best rider I have ever seen and an exceedingly good-looking man. I suppose it is to be expected that his daughter would look as if she had stepped down from Heaven or wherever angels come from!"

The Marquis walked to his desk.

"If you two are going to continue rambling on in this idiotic way," he said forcefully, "you had better go into another room, although actually I have much to discuss with Harry."

Lord Charles finished his glass of champagne.

"I don't know what I could have done to offend you, Rayburn, but I know when I am not wanted. However I would like to know what is happening about your party?"

"I have decided to postpone it until a later date," the Marquis replied.

Harry looked at him in surprise and Lord Charles remarked,

"Well, that suits me if Evelyn cannot come. I am not really interested in anybody else unless, of course, the exquisite Miss Langley will take her place!"

He was being provocative, but somehow the Marquis could not laugh as he ought to have done.

"I will let you know when I am holding another party," he said coldly, "but it will not be for some time."

"I have a feeling that you are keeping something from me," Lord Charles complained. "And if you have a party without me, Rayburn, I swear I will be an unremitting enemy. I might even call you out!"

The Marquis this time laughed, but it was not a particularly humorous sound.

"The last occasion we settled an argument that way," he pointed out, "you had your arm in a sling for three weeks."

"Well, I will think of something else," Lord Charles said, "and I promise you it will be very unpleasant!"

The Marquis was suddenly aware that Harry was frowning at him and he remembered that Lord Charles, although they were quite fond of him, was an irrepressible gossip.

He decided therefore that it would be a mistake to quarrel with him at this moment.

"Don't be a fool, Charles, you know if I have a party it would not be the same if you were not there to make everybody laugh. It is just that with a *debutante* on my hands,

I don't feel that the sort of party Harry and I were planning would be very appropriate and I can hardly go to The Castle and leave her alone here with my grandmother."

Lord Charles, who was a very good-humoured man, smiled.

"Of course not, " he said, "and if you ask me nicely I will stand back and let some of the unfledged, chinless young fools say their piece, but I warn you, Rayburn, I will not be cut out altogether!"

"I am hoping to find a responsible husband for Zia," the Marquis said heavily, "and you know as well as I do that, like me, you have no intention of marrying anyone."

"You will have to marry sometime, old man, in order to have an heir," Lord Charles replied. "As for me, you are well aware that my brother his three sons, so there is no chance of my coming into the Dukedom."

"It's a great pity," Harry smiled. "You would be the most flirtatious Duke that has ever been known, but undoubtedly the scandals that you would create would have you barred from Windsor Castle!"

"I should certainly be grateful for that mercy," Lord Charles said. "I am so sorry for all those overdressed Gentlemen-in-Waiting who have to mop the Queen's tears and listen to her eulogising hour after hour on the virtues of the late lamented Prince Consort!"

Harry and the Marquis both laughed.

At the same time they were thinking of how indiscreet Lord Charles was. The Marquis prayed that he would never know about Yasmin or the unfortunate situation that Zia had been in when he rescued her.

Because Harry was so close to the Marquis, he was aware of what he was thinking and changed the conversation by inviting Lord Charles to tell them all about the latest scandals that were being circulated in Mayfair.

As there were quite a number of them, they were still listening and laughing when the door of the study was suddenly thrown open and Zia came running in.

At that moment the Marquis was standing with his back to the fireplace while Harry and Lord Charles were sitting deep in leather armchairs.

She therefore saw only the Marquis and ran across the room to him saying,

"Look! I must show you, your Lordship, my new gown. I have never owned anything so beautiful before and there are dozens coming later for me to try on!"

She drew in her breath and went on,

"And what do you think? I have been asked to a ball tonight – my first ball and your grandmother has accepted for us all to dine with the Duchess of Bedford!"

"Then you must certainly promise me the first dance," Lord Charles said from behind her.

He obviously knew that he was behaving provocatively and he looked at the Marquis mischievously as he rose to his feet.

"Oh, I am sorry," Zia said. "I did not know that there was anybody else here."

"Let me introduce Lord Charles Fane," the Marquis said, "but I order you to disbelieve every word he speaks!"

"Now that," Lord Charles exclaimed, "is breaking every one of the Queensberry Rules! I can assure you, Miss

Langley, I am a very truthful man when I say that you are the most beautiful girl I have ever seen.".

For a moment Zia looked surprised.

"Thank you, my Lord," she said demurely, "but I always obey my Guardian."

They all laughed at this and then she said,

"I must now go and have tea with her Ladyship, but I did want you to see my gown."

"You look very nice in it," the Marquis told her.

She smiled at him and then ran from the room as Lord Charles expostulated,

"*Nice*? I ask you! A more inadequate word I have never heard! Surely, Rayburn, you have some poetry in your soul?"

"I have already told you not to spoil Zia," the Marquis replied, "and I too am now going to have tea with my grandmother and warn my Ward once again against listening to you."

"The fact that she is in your house gives you a most unfair advantage," Lord Charles complained.

But the Marquis was already leaving the room and walking down the corridor.

He had actually reached the hall when he realised that Lord Charles and Harry were behind him.

He therefore stopped just in case Lord Charles took it into his head to follow him into the drawing room where he knew that Zia would be with his grandmother.

Lord Charles was, however, taking his top hat, his gloves and his cane from the footmen and, as the butler opened the front door, he said,

"Goodbye, Rayburn, I shall see you tonight and I will certainly claim that first dance with your Ward!"

He walked out through the door without waiting for an answer and the Marquis looked at Harry.

"He is hopeless, but what can we do about him?"

"Nothing," Harry answered, "and I am sure that Zia has enough sense not to believe everything he will say to her."

The Marquis, however, was still frowning as he started to climb up the stairs.

"We have to make certain that she does not have her head turned by flibbertigibbets like Charles, but really does meet the right sort of man to make her a good husband."

There was silence as they walked up a few more stairs.

Then Harry said,

"I should have thought the answer to that was quite obvious and would certainly solve your problem,"

"What are you saying?" the Marquis demanded.

"If you want me to put it into plain English," Harry replied, "the sooner you marry the girl yourself the better!"

*

Zia thought that the ballroom of the Duchess of Bedford's house was the most beautiful scene she could ever have imagined.

The ladies in their full-skirted gowns with jewels on their heads and around their necks looked like Fairy creatures who had stepped out from a picture book.

The gentlemen were resplendent in knee breeches and silk stockings and their long-tailed coats blazing with decorations were also very impressive.

Because it was so exciting and at the same time so beautiful, she had no idea that she herself was attracting a great deal of interest and attention.

It was impossible for the Marquis, as he was so handsome, to go anywhere without being noticed.

When he entered the ballroom with Zia at his side, there was a little gasp that seemed to go up from the Dowagers sitting together who were watching the dancers.

The gentlemen standing at the end of the room deciding who should be their next partner drew in their breath when they looked at Zia.

She was wearing a gown that fortunately had required little alteration, but even so had only arrived about fifteen minutes before she had to put it on.

It was white, as was expected of a *debutante*, but ornamented with flowers that were studded with diamanté.

They encircled her *décolletage* and decorated not only her bustle but also the hem of her skirt so that she glittered with every movement she made.

The Dowager Marchioness had lent her a good number of diamond stars, which had been arranged in her hair by a skilful hairdresser.

Every man who looked at her thought that there were stars in her eyes as dazzling as those that shone amongst her shining curls.

When she came downstairs before they had left for the ball, the Marquis had admitted to himself that she was lovelier than any girl he had ever seen.

She was also, he thought, different in every way from what he expected in somebody so young.

But he told himself that Harry's idea that he should marry her was absurd and something he had no intention of doing.

While he was dressing for dinner, he had thought that Harry's suggestion of marriage was in fact quite clever.

Of course the only way he could really scotch the rumours that Yasmin was spreading about him would be to let the world know that he was to be married.

If he did announce his engagement, it would be quite fruitless after that for Yasmin to continue with her lie about carrying his child and it was doubtful in the circumstances if anyone would believe her.

Even if they did, the woman was always blamed if she was foolish enough to get into trouble without first ensuring that the man concerned would do the honourable thing and marry her.

The whole Social world was expecting the Marquis sooner or later to choose a wife.

Someone who would be a commendable Marchioness to entertain for him in the same brilliant way that his mother and grandmother had entertained the *Beau Monde*.

It was incredible that Yasmin should try so desperately to blackmail him into marriage.

Of course the Marquis was intelligent enough to realise that she could make things very uncomfortable for him if he had no direct answer to her accusations.

Harry had indeed realised very shrewdly that the only unassailable answer would be his marriage to someone else.

*

Although the Marquis had made it a rule never to dance if he could possibly help it, he started to dance with Zia as soon as they reached the ballroom.

He saw Lord Charles moving over the ballroom to take possession of her and it was something that he was determined to prevent.

"This is very exciting!" Zia enthused as they moved slowly to the music of a romantic waltz.

She did not understand why but she felt a little thrill run through her breast because the Marquis was so close and holding her.

"I thought that you would enjoy it," the Marquis replied. "Equally you will understand that you must not dance more than once with the same man and, as soon as each dance is over, you return to my grandmother and sit beside her."

"I can see through the window that there are fairy lights in the garden," Zia remarked.

Without his intending it, the Marquis's hand tightened for a moment on her small waist.

"No! No! *No!*" he declared firmly. "You will not go into the garden with anybody do you understand?"

"Of course I understand what you are telling me, my Lord, but there is no need to sound so ferocious about it!"

She smiled up at him as she spoke and the Marquis then felt that he had somehow over-reacted to the situation.

"I do *not* want you to gain a bad reputation at your very first ball!" he stressed.

"Your grandmother has told me how I am to behave," Zia said, "and I promised her I would be very good."

"I hope you will keep your promise."

"It might be – difficult if one of my – partners is very – persuasive."

For a moment the Marquis glared at her and then he realised that she was teasing him.

"For goodness sake, Zia, do be sensible," he urged her. "You must be aware that, as you are new to London and also my Ward, people will be watching and talking about you."

"Will they really?" Zia asked in surprise. "How thrilling! Was it not lucky that your grandmother and I found this beautiful gown in Bond Street?"

She lowered her voice as she added,

"Your grandmother said that I was not to tell anybody, but actually it was commissioned as a bridal gown for a Spanish Princess and now the poor seamstresses will have to sit up all night in order to create another one in time for her Wedding!"

"I expect they will be well paid for doing so," the Marquis commented cynically.

He realised as he spoke that Zia was not listening to him.

She was glancing round the room and then she said in a whisper that only he could hear,

"You are – quite right. We are being – watched! I think it's not only my gown but because – you are dancing with – someone as – unimportant as me!"

"Who has been talking to you?" the Marquis enquired.

Zia laughed.

"Your grandmother, the housekeeper, all the maids who look after me as well as Captain Blessington!"

"What has Harry been saying?" the Marquis asked sharply.

"I shall not tell you because I am sure that it would make you conceited," Zia answered, "but I do – realise that I am very – very privileged to be your Ward."

There was nothing that the Marquis could say to this and, when the dance was over, he took Zia back to his grandmother.

He had intended to go to the card room, but somehow he found it impossible not to stay in the ballroom to see what Zia was doing.

That she was a wild success at the ball was indisputable.

He noticed that every bachelor in the room was attempting to fill in her dance card, but there were many more partners than dances.

What surprised him was that unlike other *debutantes*, and there were a number of them present, Zia was talking and laughing with her partners.

Apparently their compliments were not making her feel shy.

Driving home in the carriage later with the Marquis and his grandmother she said,

"Thank you – thank you for the most – enchanting evening I have – ever spent."

"You were certainly a great success, my dear," the Dowager Marchioness answered. "I am quite sure that tomorrow there will be a great pile of invitations to similar balls and to many other entertainments."

"How – could this – happen to me?" Zia asked in a low voice. "I was so – miserable until his Lordship rescued me that I kept wondering – how I could – d-die."

"You promised me not to even think about it," the Marquis said.

"How can I help it – when I seem to have stepped into a new – world that is just like Heaven?"

"That is what I hope you will go on thinking," the Dowager Marchioness smiled.

"Do you know," Zia exclaimed as if she had just remembered, "three gentlemen, and I cannot even remember their names, asked if they could call and see me tomorrow and said that they particularly wanted to talk to me alone."

The Dowager Marchioness glanced across the carriage at her grandson.

In the light of the candle-lantern she saw that he was scowling.

"If any of them propose marriage to you," he said sharply, "you are not to accept them without asking me first."

"Propose marriage?" Zia enquired in astonishment. "Why should they do that?"

"You have to remember," the Marquis said in a hard voice, "that you have an unusually large fortune!"

There was silence for a long moment and then Zia said in a very small voice,

"I never – thought of that. Is that the reason why – so many men wanted to – dance with me?"

"No, no, of course not!" the Dowager Marchioness said quickly. "You were without exception the most beautiful and best-dressed girl in the room and they wanted to dance with you for yourself. What my grandson is telling you is that marriage is a very different thing to simply finding that you suit each other on the dance floor."

"Of course it is, but I cannot believe – any man would want to marry a girl he had – seen only once."

Again the Dowager Marchioness glanced at the Marquis.

"I think you will have so much shopping to do that you will not have time to see any of these impetuous gentlemen," he said slowly, "and I will tell the servants to turn them away."

Zia gave a little cry.

"Oh, no, please let me hear a proposal! I have often wondered what a man would say and if he really does go down on his knees as they do in novels."

The Dowager Marchioness laughed.

"You are not to be too strict as her Guardian, Rayburn. I remember my first proposal was from an elderly Colonel who was a friend of my father's and he was so emotional over it that his moustache wobbled and all I wanted to do was laugh."

The Marquis said nothing and the Dowager Marchioness added,

"Zia has to learn to handle her own affair and, when she says 'no', she must make the gentlemen, however ardent they are, believe that is what she definitely means."

As she spoke, the carriage drew up outside Oke House and the Marquis, as he was sitting on the small seat, was obliged to alight first.

As he walked into the house, he was scowling again.

*

Sister Martha heard somebody opening her bedroom door and, as she then turned from the window, she saw to her surprise that it was Zia.

"Are you awake already?" she exclaimed. "When I was told how late you came in last night, I thought that you would sleep until luncheontime."

"That is what the Dowager Marchioness expected," Zia replied, "but I am too excited to sleep and I wanted to tell you all about the ball last night."

"And I am longing to hear about it," Sister Martha said, "but first I have a confession to make to you. "

Zia looked at her curiously.

"A confession?"

"I was thinking about it last night and praying just now that I can be brave enough to tell you the truth."

"What is it?" Zia asked. "What is wrong?"

"I have lied to you," Sister Martha said and her tone was piteous.

"I – don't understand."

"I cannot go on pretending! I am not a nun and I only pretended that I was one when Father Proteus came to – the Convent."

"Is that all?" Zia asked. "Well, I think it was a very sensible thing to do."

"Do you really? You are not shocked?"

"No, of course I am not."

"I was afraid when he appeared and said that he was taking over the Convent that if I was not a nun he might send me away like the poor old women."

"It is the sort of thing he would do," Zia said.

"I had nowhere to go and Father Anthony agreed that I could stay there, but I was not to take the veil as I told him I wanted to do until I was twenty-one."

"So you thought that Father Proteus would not interfere if he believed you to be a nun."

"It was a lie and I am so ashamed of it," Martha admitted. "Father Anthony was too ill for me to explain to him what Father Proteus was doing, so I just put on the wimple and the veil of one of the nuns who was always ill in bed."

She gave a little sob that was very pathetic.

"After that everybody called me 'Sister Martha' and sometimes I forgot myself that I was just – plain Martha whom nobody wanted."

"You are not to say that again," Zia protested. "I want you and now it makes it very much easier for you to do what the Marquis suggested and teach at the school on his estate."

"When he – hears I have lied – he may not want me," Martha pointed out nervously.

"I don't think he really understands about nuns and whether they have taken the veil or not. I suppose if you were a proper nun it might be difficult, but as it is, you have just like me to forget about Father Proteus and start a new life."

Martha wiped away the tears that threatened to run down her cheeks as she answered,

"Oh, Zia, you are so kind to me and, if I could start all over again somewhere quite different, it would be very wonderful!"

"That is exactly what you are going to do."

Zia thought for a moment before she went on,

"I have a marvellous idea!"

"What is it?"

"It is only nine o'clock and the Dowager Marchioness is not being called until eleven. His Lordship has gone riding, as I asked my maid where he was when I was getting dressed."

Martha was looking at her while she spoke almost to herself and then she said,

"What we are going to do now is to go shopping! I am going to fit you out in the clothes you will wear as your real self and you can throw away that hideous garment, just as I threw away the one I had to wear."

Martha gave a little gasp and Zia went on,

"Take it off! Take it off quickly! I will give you something to wear and I will order the carriage."

She ran from the room as she spoke and came back a few minutes later with the gown that the Captain had bought for her at Falmouth.

It was too long for Martha, but they hitched it up with a belt.

Then Zia started to arrange Martha's hair, which she thought could look attractive if it was washed and curled.

She then placed on top of her head a hat that had also been bought for her at Falmouth.

Picking up the one that she had brought to wear herself and that matched her gown, she ran down the stairs with Martha.

The carriage was waiting for them and Zia told the coachman to take them to the large Emporium that she had visited yesterday with the Dowager Marchioness.

While they had been shown around, she had noticed that there were a number of gowns for young girls that the Dowager Marchioness had not considered smart enough for her.

Zia was, however, well aware that Martha would look odd in anything too smart.

If she was to teach, as the Marquis had suggested, at the village school on his estate she must not wear anything that would surprise or shock the villagers.

A footman had opened the door of the closed carriage.

The two girls climbed in, but he waited for a moment after Zia had given him the address of the Emporium and looked back at the house.

"There is no one coming with us!" she exclaimed.

"You're goin' alone, miss?"

"Just to the Emporium," Zia replied, "and it will not take long."

The footman closed the carriage door and they drove away.

"Are you quite sure you should do this?" Martha asked a little nervously. "I feel very strange dressed as I am now."

"You look very nice," Zia observed, "and, when you have clothes that really fit you, you will be surprised how attractive you will look."

She knew as Martha looked away from her that she was feeling self-conscious about her plainness and Zia told herself that she had to try and give her confidence.

But it was definitely something that she would gain amongst the children at the school who would not mind what she looked like as long as she was loving and understanding.

To take Martha's mind off herself Zia started to tell her about the ball last night.

"What did the gentlemen say who danced with you?" Martha asked.

"They paid me a lot of compliments and some of them looked at me with a 'swimmy' look in their eyes that I thought was rather ridiculous!"

"Did you dance with his Lordship?"

"He danced with me first and he dances very well," Zia replied.

Then she added,

"There was no one as handsome or smart as he was in the whole ballroom. Quite a lot of the lovely ladies in diamonds spoke to him in what I am sure my mother would have thought was an over-gushing manner."

"I expect they are in love with him!" Martha said.

Zia looked at her in surprise.

"Do you think so? But they are all married! I cannot remember their names, but one of them was a Countess, another was a Duchess and a third, who was very beautiful, was 'Lady Something-or-Other' and she said,

"'Rayburn, darling, when are you coming to see me?'"

"Did she really say that?" Martha asked.

Zia nodded.

"I thought at first that she must be one of his Lordship's relatives, but, as he moved away from her, he just said,

"'That is Lady Something-or-Other and a great number of people believe that she is the most beautiful woman in the whole of London!'"

"And was she?" Martha asked.

"I suppose she was," Zia replied. "She certainly made me feel rather plain and ordinary."

"Oh, she couldn't have!" Martha exclaimed. "You're lovely and the maids say you are the most beautiful girl who has ever been at Oke House!"

"Did they really say that?" Zia asked with interest.

"They did. But they also said that the Lady Yasmin his Lordship's been meeting up to now is very beautiful."

Zia thought and then she said,

"I don't think that anyone called 'Yasmin' was there last night."

"No, she's in France," Martha explained. "I heard the housekeeper tell Amy, the maid who looks after me, that her husband was very ill."

She thought for a moment and then she said,

"Lady Caton, that is what her name is, Yasmin Caton! And the way that they talked it sounded as if his Lordship is infatuated with her."

Zia looked at her.

She had not until now thought of the Marquis as being infatuated with anybody.

Now she told herself that she must be very stupid.

Of course, seeing how handsome he was and how the lovely ladies had clustered round him last night, should have made her aware that they were all enamoured with him.

It was the same way, she thought now, that her mother had told her that the ladies would sometimes pursue her father.

"You are too good-looking, darling," she had said to him once, "and I am always afraid I shall lose you."

"How could you possibly think anything like that?" the Colonel had replied. "There is not another woman as lovely as you in the world. From the moment I first saw you, you stole my heart away and I can assure you that it is yours from now to Eternity."

Her mother had laughed and Zia remembered the expression of happiness that there had been in her eyes.

She could picture now the way she had lifted her lips so that her father could kiss her.

'I want someone to love me like that,' she thought.

She knew that it was something that she could never feel towards any of the young men who had asked last night if they could call on her this afternoon.

At the same time she knew that she would have been very foolish not to realise how handsome, attractive and fascinating the Marquis was.

'When I talked to him in the yacht,' she mused, 'I was not thinking of him as a man, but as if he was the Archangel Michael who had come down from Heaven to save me from the wickedness of Father Proteus.'

She wondered what Lady Caton would have done if she had been in her place on *The Unicorn*.

Then, before she could find a satisfactory answer, they had arrived at the Emporium.

Zia had learnt quite a lot from the way that the Dowager Marchioness had behaved.

She sent for the Manageress and said to her,

"I am Miss Zia Langley who came in here yesterday with the Dowager Marchioness of Okehampton."

"Yes, yes, miss, I remember it well," the Manageress replied.

"I have brought this young lady with me who is a friend of mine," Zia said indicating Martha, "and I want her dressed completely from head to foot. Her clothes have all been lost in an accident and she has therefore nothing to wear but the dress I have lent her, which, as you can see, does not fit her."

"Oh, dear, what a catastrophe!" the Manageress exclaimed. "But I am sure we can find what the young lady desires."

"Now what she wants," Zia said firmly, "are clothes that she can wear in the country that will not be ostentatious, if you understand what I mean. She is going to live very quietly helping a friend of his Lordship's to run a school."

As she spoke, she saw by the expression on the Manageress's face that she understood exactly what she was trying to say to her.

"We have not much time," Zia went on, "and, if we can have my friend fitted out with one or two gowns that she can wear immediately, then the rest of the things can be sent as quickly as possible to Oke House."

It was an order that was exactly after the Manageress's heart.

In a very short while Martha was fitted out in a slimmer gown that was pretty but much plainer and less voluminous than the one that Zia was wearing.

There was a hat to match it and even shoes and stockings, which came from another part of the Emporium.

Zia kept an eye on the clock, thinking perhaps that the Dowager Marchioness might wish to do something with her before luncheon.

It was, however, getting on towards noon when they went outside to where the carriage was waiting.

Before they left the Manageress promised to pack up everything that they had chosen and send it round to Oke House.

"Thank you very much," Zia said to her as the footman jumped down from the box to open the door for her.

"It has been a real pleasure, miss, and I hope I shall see you here again," the Manageress replied.

"I am sure you will," Zia smiled.

As she went through the Emporium door and out onto the pavement, there was a strong wind blowing down the street and she put up her hand to hold onto her hat.

It prevented her from seeing anything but her way to the carriage and then she stepped inside it.

As she did so, the door was slammed to.

She looked back in astonishment to see Martha staggering and then falling down on the pavement as if somebody had struck her.

But before she could see clearly what had occurred the horses started off and she was aware that the footman who had slammed the door had now jumped up onto the box.

She could not understand what was happening.

Then she looked through the glass window over the small seat that faced her.

She could see the coachman who was driving the carriage and the footman sitting beside him.

She raised her hand to knock urgently on the window to let them know that they had left Martha behind.

As she did so, the footman, wearing what she saw was the livery of the Marquis, turned round to look down at her.

It was then that she saw his face and there was a scar that ran from his forehead into his eyebrow.

At the sight of him she gave a scream of horror and collapsed onto the back seat of the carriage.

Her heart was beating frantically with fear.

The footman looking at her was somebody she could not fail to recognise!

He was Father Proteus's man from the Convent, Saul!

CHAPTER SIX

The Marquis, who had been riding in Hyde Park with Harry, left him at the end of Park Lane.

"I will see you tonight," Harry said, "but now I have to hurry as I am having luncheon with the Duchess."

"She will be annoyed if you are late," the Marquis remarked.

"1 know," Harry replied ruefully, "but it will be worth it to have had the best ride I have had for many a month."

The Marquis was smiling as he trotted slowly up Park Lane towards his own house.

He found himself looking forward to seeing Zia and hearing if she had enjoyed the ball last night.

As his grandmother had related, she had been an undoubted success.

He thought it extraordinary that a girl who had lived such a sheltered life should step into the most sophisticated Society in Europe and manage to captivate everyone who saw her.

She was not shy, gauche or anything else that he might have expected a young girl to be.

'She is certainly original,' he told himself and knew that quite a few men were envying him for being her Guardian.

A groom was waiting for him outside the front door of Oke House and he dismounted and patted his horse as if to thank him for a good ride.

Then he walked in through the front door, which had been opened for him by a footman.

To his amazement he found that the hall was filled with people.

There was his secretary Mr. Barrett, the housekeeper, his coachman and the footman peculiarly dressed and several maidservants.

There was also a young woman in a pretty gown whom he did not recognise at once as being Sister Martha.

As he appeared, they all stopped and stared at him in a way that told him without words that something was very wrong.

"What is it? What has happened?" he asked. "Why are you all here?"

He spoke to Mr. Barrett who exclaimed,

"Thank goodness you have returned, my Lord!"

"What can be the matter?" the Marquis asked.

"Miss Zia has been kidnapped!"

For a moment the Marquis was too astonished to speak. Then he demanded,

"When and by whom?"

He knew the answer, but it was something he wanted to hear from the people staring at him.

His coachman, Dobson, a middle-aged man who had been in service with his father and was excellent with horses, came from among the crowd.

"It were like this, my Lord," he began, "it weren't my fault, nor Ben's – "

"Suppose you start at the beginning," the Marquis suggested quietly.

His voice was under control and he appeared to be outwardly at ease.

At the same time his anger was rising as he realised that this was something he should have anticipated and prevented.

"I think you should know," Mr. Barrett interrupted, "that Miss Zia left the house soon after nine o'clock this morning taking Sister Martha with her."

He glanced at Martha, who was standing near him with a handkerchief held to her eyes.

"Who else went with you?" the Marquis asked her.

"No one – my Lord."

"Where did you go?"

She took the handkerchief from her eyes to say,

"Zia came into my bedroom and – when I told her that I was not really a nun, she said that she would find me – the right clothes so that I-I could teach in the school your Lordship – spoke about."

As she was sobbing, her words were almost incoherent, but the Marquis understood.

"So you went shopping alone in one of my carriages?"

"Y-yes, my Lord, and then Saul took her away!"

As if the Marquis did not quite follow the sequence of events, he looked at Dobson for a further explanation and he reported,

"When we reached the Emporium, my Lord, Miss Zia said as she'd be about an hour and an 'alf, so I takes the horses under the shade of the trees in the square that's just behind Bond Street."

The Marquis nodded and Dobson went on,

"Ben and I were just sittin' talkin' in the shade when we was suddenly hauled off the box by two men, one of them with a big scar on 'is face."

"That was Saul!" Martha cried. "And he hit me when I tried to get into the carriage with Zia."

The Marquis ignored the interruption and said to Dobson,

"After they had pulled you from the carriage, what did they do?"

"They took our coats and 'ats, my Lord, and tied us up to a tree and then drove off with the carriage."

It seemed so incredible that for a moment the Marquis could only stare at his coachman.

Then Martha, as if she realised that she must tell him the rest of the story, moved a little nearer to him and said,

"We came out of the shop and Zia climbed into the carriage, but, when I would have joined her, Saul hit me so that I fell down onto the pavement and then – he jumped up on the box and they drove off at speed."

She burst into tears as she sobbed,

"Father Proteus has her again! Oh – save her, my Lord, *save her*!"

The Marquis turned and looked at the other people in the hall.

"Has anybody anything to add to this story?" he asked them.

There was no answer and Mr. Barrett said,

"I think that is everything we know, my Lord."

"Very well," the Marquis murmured. "Come with me, Barrett, and we will see what can be done. Everybody else can go back to their duties."

He walked towards the study and Mr. Barrett followed him.

When his secretary had closed the door, the Marquis enquired,

"Has her Ladyship been told about this?"

"Yes, my Lord, and she is very upset and so has stayed in bed."

"That is sensible at any rate," the Marquis commented.

He sat down at his desk.

"Now, Barrett, what are we going to do?"

"I really have no idea, my Lord," Mr. Barrett replied, "except to send for the Police."

"If we do," the Marquis said after a moment's pause, "the whole story will undoubtedly get into the newspapers."

Mr. Barrett said nothing.

The Marquis stared in front of him thinking furiously that Zia was again in the power of a dangerous man and somehow he had to save her.

He rose to walk slowly to the window while he was thinking.

As he looked out with unseeing eyes at the sunshine in the garden, he felt as if his whole comfortable world had unexpectedly fallen about his ears.

Why had he not anticipated that Proteus instead of acknowledging defeat as he might have expected, would not give up until he had Zia's money in his greedy hands?

The Marquis was quite certain that this would now be a case of ransom and Proteus was in a strong position to demand an outrageously large sum of money for the return of Zia.

He knew that what he had to do now was to wait until the ransom note arrived.

Yet every nerve in his body was crying out for him to save Zia before she suffered any more than she was already.

'Why did I not know? Why did I not *guess*,' he asked himself, 'that this might happen?'

He was furiously angry that he should have been so foolish as not to anticipate the way a criminal's mind would work.

'I have to do something!' the Marquis insisted to himself.

But the only thing he could think was that London was a very large place.

And if, as he suspected, Proteus intended to hide Zia until the money was in his hands, it would be completely impossible for anyone to find her.

He assumed that the fake Priest would not play the same game of hiding in a Convent or any other Religious institution.

And yet he might have access to one whose doors were closed to the surveillance of the public.

What it all amounted to, the Marquis acknowledged to himself, was that he had no clue and no idea where Zia might be.

Later the horses and carriage might turn up, but Proteus would take very good care that they were found far away from any secret place where he held Zia.

There was a note of despair in the Marquis's voice when, after being silent for a long time, he said,

"There must be something we can do."

"That is what I have been telling myself, my Lord," Mr. Barrett replied. "Maybe it would be possible to hire a detective, or several of them, whom we could swear to secrecy."

"We will inevitably sooner or later have to call in the Police," the Marquis replied, "and I have no wish to do so until Zia is safely home."

The way he spoke made Mr. Barrett fully aware that the Marquis was thinking that, if the Police threatened Proteus, he might in desperation, or perhaps revenge, kill his captive.

There was silence again and, surprised at himself for doing so, the Marquis was actually praying that by some miracle he could gain some idea of where Zia might have been taken.

The door opened and the butler walked in,

"There's a man here, my Lord, from *The Unicorn*, says his name's Winton and he wishes to see your Lordship and I thinks, although I may be wrong, it concerns Miss Zia."

The Marquis turned round quickly.

"Winton!" he exclaimed. "Send him in!"

As he waited, he looked at Mr. Barrett, although neither of them spoke.

The Marquis was thinking that it was impossible that Winton could know anything.

His instructions after he had left *The Unicorn* were for it to proceed to Greenwich, where they were to wait until he required the yacht again.

It seemed to him a long time, although it was actually only two or three minutes before Winton, who had called at the kitchen door, came into the study.

He was in uniform and was holding his cap in his hand.

He was looking somewhat over-awed until he saw the Marquis and then there was a grin on his face as he said,

"Good-day, my Lord."

"I understand you have something to tell me," the Marquis said as if he could not waste any time.

"I have, my Lord." Winton replied. "And it be about Miss Langley."

The Marquis drew in his breath.

He walked to his desk and indicated a chair on the other side of it before he said,

"Sit down and tell me everything you know."

"Well, it's like this, my Lord," Winton replied, sitting on the edge of his chair. "After your Lordship left us, we moved *The Unicorn* a little way down river as the Captain needed some vittles and so he sends ashore for them. We also needed some paint, as your Lordship'll remember, to touch up the yacht where it was marked on the starboard side."

"Yes, I remember," the Marquis murmured impatiently.

Only by a tremendous effort at self-control did he force himself not to shout at Winton to get to the point.

"Well, I was on deck, my Lord," Winton went on, "seein' them urchins as was playin' about didn't make a nuisance of themselves on the bank when a little way down river I spots a man I'd seen afore."

"Who was it?" the Marquis asked. "And where had you seen him?"

"At the Convent, my Lord, the one you took me to."

"You are sure that is where you saw him?"

"Yes, my Lord. I sees him there lookin' out of the window at me and I noticed him particular-like, because he had a scar on his forehead, runnin' down into his eyebrow it was."

"Yes, *yes*!" the Marquis said. "His name is 'Saul'."

"I sees him again," Winton went on, "when he runs out of the gate as we were leavin' with Miss Langley and your Lordship tells me to fire the pistol over their heads."

Winton paused for breath and the Marquis asked,

"And you saw him again today on the river?"

"Yes, my Lord. Him and another man was climbin' into a boat as was bein' rowed by two others."

"A boat!" the Marquis exclaimed.

"Yes, my Lord."

"And they were alone?"

"No, my Lord. They had a woman with them. I couldn't see her clearly, not then, but – "

"Go on!" the Marquis urged him again.

"Because I were curious, my Lord, I leaves Harper – you knows Harper, my Lord?"

"Yes, yes," the Marquis answered. "Go on with what you were saying."

"I walks down to see where they was a-goin' and, as they gets into midstream, I then recognises the lady as is with them. It were Miss Langley, my Lord!"

"You are quite sure?" Mr. Barrett enquired as if he could keep silent no longer.

Winton turned towards Mr. Barrett.

"Yes, sir, I were quite sure it be Miss Langley. She had no hat on her head so I could see her quite clear-like."

"You watched them?" the Marquis asked. "Where did they go?"

"They goes straight across the river, my Lord, and downstream for a short way and then into a houseboat."

"You are quite certain it was a houseboat, Winton?"

"Oh, yes, my Lord, and there was only one at that particular point on the Thames, lyin' by some bushes and a pretty tumbledown affair it be and all, needin' paint. Not the sort of boat as your Lordship'd give a second glance to!"

"A houseboat!" the Marquis exclaimed. "And that is where Miss Langley is now?"

"They takes her ashore, my Lord, and I were certain after that they takes her aboard the houseboat."

The Marquis put his hand to his head as if it helped him to think more clearly.

"You have done me a great service, Winton, and you will be amply rewarded. "Now I want you to have something to eat while I talk to Mr. Barrett and decide how we will rescue Miss Langley."

As he rose to his feet, Winton rose too and then he said,

"You'll let me in on it, my Lord? You knows I can be trusted with a pistol – "

"I promise you shall be in on it," the Marquis assured him. "Just give me time to work out my plan of campaign."

Mr. Barrett had already rung the bell for him and the door opened almost immediately.

"See that Winton is given something substantial to eat," the Marquis said to the butler, "and I will send for him a little later."

"Very good, my Lord."

The Marquis did not say anything more until Winton had left the room.

He was telling himself that, quite incredibly, his prayer had been answered and by a miracle he now knew where Zia was.

*

Zia was very afraid.

She had been terrified when the carriage had driven away with her from the Emporium and she knew at once that she had been captured by Father Proteus's men.

She tried to think of some way that she could throw herself out of the carriage.

But the horses were travelling as fast as they could in the traffic and she was certain that, if she did try to get out, she would fall under the wheels.

Even if she was not injured, Saul would catch her before she could run away and he might then hit her as he had just hit Martha.

Sitting on the back seat and supporting herself because they were travelling so fast, she thought how stupid she had been to go shopping with Martha without taking anybody with them.

Then she thought that even if the housekeeper or a maid had come with them, they would have been powerless to prevent her from being kidnapped.

In some frightening manner the Marquis's coachman and footman had been disposed of and Saul and another of Father Proteus's men were now driving the carriage.

She sat trembling, realising that they had now left the shops behind and were entering a poorer and dirtier part of the City.

She caught a sudden glimpse of water and realised that the River Thames was just ahead of them.

Then she had the terrifying feeling that Father Proteus was going to take her away in a ship to a foreign country.

If he did, she knew that no one would ever find her again, not even the Marquis.

As she thought of him, her whole being cried out towards him to save her.

He had saved her once and she remembered how exciting it had been as he had driven her away from the Convent and she had thought joyously that she was rid of the evil Father Proteus forever.

At the back of her mind she had always been afraid that she would never be able to escape from the Convent and Father Proteus.

Now she was back in his clutches and she knew that he would never be satisfied until he had control of, if not all her money, then a great deal of it.

'What can I do?' she asked herself desperately.

Then she was praying to the Marquis to come once again to her rescue.

'Save – me! *Save – me*,' she cried in her heart, 'as – only – *you* can do!'

The carriage came to a standstill and she realised that they were on a road that bordered a river and it must be the River Thames.

She wondered if she jumped out and threw herself into the Thames whether she would be able to escape.

She could swim because her father had taught her, but she knew that it would be very difficult in the full-skirted gown she was wearing.

She was more likely to sink and be drowned.

The door of the carriage was then pulled open and Saul was leering at her with an evil expression in his eyes under the scar that disfigured his forehead.

"Come on!" he ordered. "You've 'ad a nice ride and now we're takin' you on the water!"

Zia realised that it was no use arguing with him.

As he spoke, he was pulling off the livery coat that he had taken from the Marquis's servants and he flung it into the carriage.

The coachman, whom she recognised as a man who had been at the Convent and who was called 'Mark', threw his after it.

Then the two men in their shirtsleeves each took one of her arms and marched her down to the water's edge.

As they did so, she heard the carriage drive away and hoped that whoever had taken it would be kind to the Marquis's fine horses.

Then she saw below her that there was a rowing boat in which the other two men who had been at the Convent were waiting.

"'Ere she be now," Saul called out to them. "And a good deal more fancy to look at than when we last sees 'er!"

He pushed Zia into the boat and then the two men who were already in it started to row across the river.

There was a strong current and Zia wondered if they would be swept away and whether if the boat capsized perhaps she would have a chance of running away from them.

With a great deal of puffing and blowing they managed to reach calmer waters and she saw ahead of them what appeared to be a very dilapidated houseboat.

It was moored to a rough bank and at first she could not believe that this was their destination.

Then, as they pulled the boat to the bank and dragged her out onto the rough ground, she knew that this improbable hiding place was where she was to be imprisoned.

For a moment she thought of screaming and shouting and making one desperate dash for freedom.

Then, as she gazed at the hard unbuilt-on ground that the houseboat was moored against, she saw that this was a lonely spot where there were no wharfs and in consequence very few people.

If she screamed as loud as she could, who would hear her?

If anyone did, who was likely to confront Saul and Mark and the other two men who looked as tough and pugnacious as they did?

But she had, as it happened, little time for thought.

The men pulled her up the rickety gangplank and onto the deck, taking her through a dilapidated door into what she supposed was the Saloon.

Sitting in an armchair, his leg in a splint, was Father Proteus, a bottle of brandy beside him.

At the sight of him, Zia felt herself shiver.

She could see as she looked at him how furious he was that she had escaped.

"'Ere she be!" Saul said brightly.

"You've been a devil of a long time!" Father Proteus complained. "Does anyone know you've brought her here?"

"Not unless they're birds in the sky!" Saul replied. "And Dixon's taken off the 'orses."

"What has he done with them?" Father Proteus asked.

"'E'll sell 'em soon as 'e gets the chance and put the carriage in a scrapyard."

Zia closed her eyes.

She thought of how the Marquis would mind his horses, which he was so proud of, being sold to some buyer who might overwork them or worse still be cruel to them.

Then, as Father Proteus's eyes were on her, she could only think of herself.

"A fine dance you've led me, my girl!" he began as he glared at her. "But you'll pay for it, just as you'll pay for that damnable Guardian of yours cracking up my leg!"

He shouted the words at her.

Then, as if he hated the very sight of her, he ordered,

"Take her below and lock her in. Take away her gown and shoes just in case she tries to escape."

"She won't be able to do that!" Saul smirked.

He was laughing at the idea and Zia knew that he was gloating over the fact that she was helpless and there was nothing she could do about it.

He had seized Zia by the arm, digging his fingers into the softness of her skin.

"Now listen," Father Proteus said as if a sudden thought struck him, "you are going to write a letter to your Guardian telling him that, unless he pays every penny I ask of him, I'll kill you. Do you understand?"

With an effort Zia managed to respond defiantly,

"If you kill me as you killed that other girl at the Convert, you will be hanged!"

Father Proteus laughed and it was a very unpleasant sound.

"Do you suppose I am as stupid as you are?" he asked. "If we put you in the Thames and hold your head down, you'll float away on the tide and be many miles from here before somebody pulls your dead limp body out of the water."

The way he spoke made Zia feel as if she must scream and go on screaming, but with a superhuman effort she pressed her lips together and said nothing.

"Take her away!" Father Proteus ordered. "It makes me sick to look at her!"

Saul dragged Zia towards the door and Father Proteus roared,

"Mark, bring another bottle of brandy! This damned leg is hurting like all the fires of Satan!"

Saul pulled Zia down the companionway, where the steps were cracked and broken, to the lower deck of the houseboat.

There was a passage with several doors opening out of it that she could see were cabins.

He took her to one near the stern that looked out onto the river.

She knew it was because he had no intention of letting her think that she might climb through a porthole onto dry land.

He stood for a moment looking round the very small cabin.

As if he wanted to hurt her, he gave her a push in the middle of her back that sent her sprawling onto a narrow iron bedstead that stood in the centre of the cabin.

"Now you behave yourself," be warned, "or I promise you, you'll suffer worse than 'his Nibs' be!"

It was a threat that instinctively made Zia cringe away from him.

He laughed and it was a harsh sound that seemed to echo round the small cabin and then he left.

She heard him close the door behind him and lock it and she had the idea that it was a new lock that had been specially put there to keep her from escaping.

Just as she thought that she was rid of him, she heard the key turn again and he came back.

"You 'eard what the old man said," he leered. "Give us your dress and your shoes!"

"I will put them outside the door when I have taken them off," Zia replied.

"Shy, are you?" Saul sniggered. "I'll 'elp you, if you can't manage."

"Wait outside the door!" Zia said.

She spoke firmly, looking at him defiantly and for one terrifying moment she thought that he would not do as she demanded.

Then, as if he felt that it was a mistake to molest her, he went from the cabin and she knew that he would be waiting outside.

Quickly, because she was afraid that he might come back in again and try to touch her, she took off the beautiful gown that she had put on to go shopping with Martha.

As it fell to the floor, she picked it up with her shoes and, opening the door as short a way as possible, handed them through.

She saw Saul's dirty hands come out to take them.

"You can 'ave this back when you've paid for it," he jeered.

She slammed the door in his face as he laughed.

Once again the key was turned in the lock and Zia sank down on the bed feeling that she must be the most terrified woman in the whole world.

Not even the Marquis would be able to find her and she was in the power of men who would not hesitate to kill her if it would save their skins.

She wanted to beat on the wall and to cry out despairingly, but her sixth sense told her that it would be no help.

Somehow, and she was not even certain why, she recognised that she had to keep her wits about her.

She went over to the porthole to look out on the river.

The River Thames was very wide at this particular point and she could see on the other side of the river that there were only a few wharfs and industrial buildings, but no houses for human habitation.

'Even if I was able to signal,' she thought, 'nobody would be there to see it and Saul and the other men would not hesitate to attack me if they knew what I was doing.'

She went from the porthole to sit on the bed.

It contained an old faded mattress that the stuffing was escaping from in a number of places and the cover was torn and stained. There were two thin blankets, which were also none too clean.

Otherwise the cabin was empty and looked as if it had been so for a long time.

'I could die here and – nobody would ever be aware of it,' Zia said forlornly to herself.

Then, almost as if a voice told her so, she knew that her father and mother would know and, whatever else happened, they would never forget her.

'Help me – Papa,' she prayed. 'You have been in – dangerous situations in your life – but I never thought it would ever – happen to me.'

Then once again she knew that the only one who could save her was the Marquis.

He had saved her from the Convent when she had thought that she was utterly lost and abandoned.

She was certain that, when Father Proteus had got hold of her money as he intended, she would die in some strange accident that no one could prove was murder.

Father Proteus would also wish to kill her because he blamed her for being instrumental in injuring his leg.

She was sure that, when he had threatened her with drowning, he was already planning that was what he would do once her money was in his hands.

She started to pray again fervently, praying to her father, her mother and the Marquis.

'Save me – *save – me*!'

It was a cry that not only came from her heart but from her soul.

*

It was now late in the day and outside the sun was sinking as Zia heard footsteps coming below.

She had heard the voices of the men, although they had not been talking loudly for fear of drawing attention to themselves.

Now the key turned in the lock and, when the door opened, it was Mark who stood there.

He had a tray in his hand and she saw that on it was food of some sort and a cup and saucer.

He put the tray down on the end of the bed and said,

"Father Proteus says, although he ain't a Father no longer, we've got to keep you alive till you've writ a letter for your money, so eat up, otherwise one of us'll have to feed you!"

He waited for Zia to reply and, when she said nothing, he went on,

"Sulky, are you? Well, we'll 'ave to think of some way of cheerin' you up, won't we?"

He gave her a look that made her shiver and then he went from the cabin locking the door after him.

She looked at the food on the tray thinking that she was really far too frightened and unhappy to be hungry.

There were some slices of cold meat that did not look at all appetising on a cracked plate and a piece of bread from a cottage loaf that had obviously been newly baked.

To eat with it on the same plate as the meat was a pat of butter and a piece of rather evil-smelling cheese.

In the cup there was coffee, which at least smelt reasonably fragrant.

She remembered then how Father Proteus, when he had been at the Convent, drank a great deal of coffee and she reckoned that, if nothing else, this at least would be drinkable.

She ate a little of the bread and butter, but drank all the coffee.

Then she put the tray down near the door so that whoever fetched it would not have to come far into the cabin.

By now it was dusk and a little while later she heard sounds that at first terrified her.

Then she realised that the men were carrying the injured Father Proteus down the rickety companionway to a cabin not far from hers.

Whenever they hurt his leg with the movements they made, he swore oaths that she had never heard before, but was quite certain were lewd and vulgar.

She also had the idea from the sound of the men's voices that they had all had a great deal to drink.

Because she was frightened that they might come into her cabin, she held her breath and her whole body was tense until she heard Saul say,

"Now you knows what you've got to do. We all sleeps up top and Mark and Mike'll take the first watch while Joseph and me takes the second."

"I'm sleepy," she heard Mark complaining.

"You'd better not let the old man hear you say that," Saul replied.

The other man, Joseph, said something unpleasant that made them all laugh and then they climbed up on deck and Zia gave a sigh of relief.

She supposed that she should try to sleep on the dreadful bed.

Tomorrow, when she had to write the letter to ask for her ransom, she might be able, if she was clever, to put some clue in it as to where she was being held.

Then she knew despairingly that whatever she wrote would be read and re-read by Father Proteus to be quite certain that she had not betrayed them.

'Help me – Papa – *help me*!' she prayed even more fervently.

Then she thought again of the Marquis.

She felt as if she could see him as he had looked last night, so smart, so handsome and so irresistible to all the ladies who had clustered round him.

Then she remembered how she had danced with him and how exciting it had been to be close to him with his hand on her waist.

'If only he was – here now,' she whispered to herself.

As she spoke, her heart throbbed and a little thrill ran through her.

Then she knew that she *loved* him – and had done so ever since they had been together on his yacht.

*

The Marquis had made his plans very carefully.

He was desperately afraid, however, that if anything went wrong Zia might be hurt or even worse.

As he drove down to the river with Winton in his closed carriage, his mind was working like a well-oiled machine to make absolutely certain that he had thought of every possible detail.

When he went aboard *The Unicorn*, he had called the Captain and the crew into the Saloon.

He told them what had happened and what he had decided to do.

He then went on,

"We are not dealing with ordinary criminals, but extremely clever ones. One slip, one mistake and we shall fail to rescue Miss Langley."

"I assure you, my Lord," the Captain said, "that your orders will be carried out and, as you well know, several of the men aboard *The Unicorn* have served in the Royal Navy."

"I know," the Marquis said, "and I am relying on them, Captain, as I am on you, to help me save Miss Zia from men who every one of them should be behind bars while the head of the gang should undoubtedly be hanged."

The Marquis then stayed aboard *The Unicorn* until one-thirty in the morning.

Silently, leaving only two of the older members of the crew to keep watch, the rest set out.

Each man was aware of his part in a plan of attack that they all recognised could only have been thought out by someone as astute as the Marquis.

Six of the seamen landed up-river, some distance from the houseboat and so well out of sight.

They then approached the houseboat in single file, moving through the unbuilt-on ground where there were a number of rough bushes that afforded a certain amount of cover.

. When they were nearer the houseboat, Winton and another seaman crawled forward cautiously, making no sound so that the two men on watch on the houseboat had no idea of their presence.

Saul and Joseph were not only inebriated but also sleepy.

They had gone up on deck as they had been told to do and Saul was sitting down near the gangplank with his back against the wall of the Saloon and his eyes kept closing.

Joseph in the bow of the ship had lain down on deck and was so drunk as to be almost unconscious.

Neither of the so-called guards was aware that Winton and the man with him had cut the ropes that held the houseboat to the bank.

Creeping along the muddy side of the river up to their knees in water, four other seamen started to push the houseboat downstream.

The tide was going out and it was easy with their combined strength to move the boat away from the bank in what at first was only a few feet of water.

Then, as it was caught by the current, it swung out at about ten feet from dry land.

It was then that Winton, standing up, shouted out,

"Hey, Mister. Your boat's afloat!"

His voice aroused Saul who then looked up, saw a dark figure on the bank and for some seconds could not realise what was happening.

Then Winton called out,

"Throw us your rope and I'll pull you back!"

As Winton was shouting, two other seamen came to his side and Saul's cries for help brought Mark, Joseph and Jacob to assist him.

Nobody noticed in the dark that the seamen from the yacht were dripping wet below the waist. They were much too intent on throwing the ropes that were lying in the stern of the houseboat onto the shore.

It was extraordinary how difficult it seemed to be and how clumsy Winton and the other two men with him were at catching the ropes.

They seemed to slip through their hands so that they had to be thrown again and again.

Winton was joined by more men making six, also wet, but they were no more successful than the others.

The noise of the men shouting,

"'Ere, catch this!"

"Look out!"

"'Ere's another!" seemed to fill the air.

As the Marquis swam to the other side of the houseboat, he was quite sure that nobody would notice him.

He knew that Zia would be locked in one of the cabins and he wasted no time by looking through the portholes.

Instead he climbed with the expertise of an athlete up the side of the rickety houseboat and onto the deck that faced the Thames.

No one was there to see him.

He went to the door on the opposite side to where the men were shouting at each other and slipped down the companionway.

Although it was dark, he managed by the lights that had been left burning in the Saloon to see the cabin doors.

He felt with his hands the first one he came to, realising as he tried the handle that the door was unlocked and moved quickly away.

He could hear somebody shouting in one cabin and realised that it was Father Proteus.

He was calling for one of his men to come and tell him what was happening.

Then the Marquis's hand encountered a strong lock and a key and he realised that he had found whom he was seeking.

He turned the key and pulled open the door.

Zia, who had been aroused by all the noise, was sitting up against the back of the bed.

For a moment, as the door opened and she saw the shadow of a man, she thought that it was Saul.

She was so frightened that, although she opened her mouth to scream, no sound came.

Then her instinct told her who it was.

As the Marquis's arms went out towards her, she threw herself against him and put her arms around his neck like a child who had been frightened by the dark.

"It is – *you* – !" she managed to almost scream.

Then his lips were on hers to silence the words.

As he kissed her, she felt as if the sky had opened and a light enveloped them both.

Her whole body seemed to come alive.

Then, when the Marquis picked her up in his arms, she realised that he was wet through and she knew how he had reached her.

Yet she held herself close against him as he carried her up the companionway and out onto the deck that faced the river.

"You are quite safe," he whispered, "there is a boat below."

As he lowered her down the side, strong arms reached up to take her from him.

The boat was manned by three seamen and, as the Marquis climbed into it, he joined Zia in the stern and they pulled away from the houseboat.

He put his arm around her to hold her against him and because she felt that he had lifted her up to Heaven, she hid her face against his wet shoulder.

He did not speak and they were halfway across the Thames before he said,

"You are safe now and this shall never happen to you again."

She did not answer, but he could feel her quivering against him.

As she did so, he vowed to himself to protect her, to keep her safe and to love her for the rest of his life.

'How can I have been such a fool as to lose her?' he had asked himself a thousand times while he and his crew were waiting to go into action.

Now he had won a victory, but the only thing that really mattered was that Zia was with him again.

CHAPTER SEVEN

As the rowing boat reached the riverbank, the clouds unexpectedly rolled away.

It had been a dark night, but now the moon was shining and, as the Marquis picked up Zia in his arms and carried her off the boat, he looked back.

He could see now more clearly than he had been able to do before that the houseboat had drifted almost to the middle of the river.

It was dipping heavily at the stern and the Marquis knew that it was filling with water.

On his orders the seamen who had pushed it away from the bank had, once he had rowed away with Zia, made a hole just below the water level.

He was certain that it would not be a difficult thing to do as the houseboat was so dilapidated.

Now he calculated that the stern would be taking in water and he thought already it must be deep in the cabin where Proteus was.

He could see quite clearly his own men on the bank and the four men of the gang on the houseboat must have jumped overboard and were struggling to reach land.

Two were now coming out of the water and would be seized by his men as soon as they landed.

The other two were in difficulties and he suspected that they could not swim.

If they were to drown as well as Father Proteus, it would be a good thing and would save any Court proceedings that might be brought against them by the Police.

The Marquis's carriage was waiting and having deposited Zia on the back seat, he stood for a moment looking again at the houseboat.

Now it was definitely sinking and he was sure that it was just a question of time, perhaps five or ten minutes, before it disappeared altogether.

This meant that Proteus could never threaten Zia again.

He climbed into the carriage and, as a footman put a rug over his knees, he realised that Zia had crossed her hands over her breasts.

For the first time he noticed that she was wearing only a silk chemise and a petticoat.

Very gently he wrapped the rug around her like a shawl. Then, as the carriage moved off, she looked up at him and exclaimed in a lilting voice,

"*You* – saved – me!"

He put his arm around her and replied,

"You are safe, my darling, and I shall never forgive myself for not anticipating that this might happen."

"I prayed that – you would save me – and I am sure that Papa – helped you to do so."

"I am sure he did," the Marquis replied, "but all that matters for the moment is that you are safe."

He pulled her a little closer to him and then he said,

"I am afraid I have made you wet."

"It does not matter. I just want to be really sure that you are here."

She put her hand on his shoulder as if to reassure her and he breathed gently,

"There is a better way of making sure."

As he spoke, his lips came down on hers.

To Zia it was what she had wanted and exactly what she had been longing for.

She had been afraid when they were in the boat that he had kissed her merely to prevent her from speaking.

Now sensations that she had never known before were rippling through her body and she felt her love rising up towards him almost like the waves of the sea.

'I love you – *I love you*!' she wanted to say, but it was impossible to speak.

As the Marquis kissed her and went on kissing her with slow passionate kisses, it made her feel strongly as if she was part of him and that they could never be separated.

All she knew was that it was as if a blinding light from Heaven surrounded them both and it made her quiver with the intensity of it.

She had a strange feeling that the Marquis was feeling the same.

They had driven a long way before he said,

"Because I don't want you ever again to be worried as I know you are at this moment, the man you called 'Proteus' has been drowned!"

There was a little pause as if Zia found it hard to think of anything except the ecstasy he had given her.

Then she asked in a low voice,

"In the – houseboat?"

"There was nothing to prevent it from sinking to the bottom of the river," the Marquis related.

Zia drew in her breath.

"Perhaps it is – wrong to be glad – but now I need – no longer be afraid."

"You will never be again," the Marquis said, "and to make sure of it, how soon will you marry me, my precious darling?"

They were passing some lights and, as she looked up at him, he could see the expression of radiance on her face.

Then, as he waited, once again she hid her face against his shoulder.

"You – cannot really want to – *marry* me," she whispered.

"I want it more than I have ever wanted anything in my life before," the Marquis replied, "and, my darling, no one can accuse me of being a fortune-hunter!"

"I-I was not thinking of that, but perhaps I will – bore you and you would be – happier with one of the – beautiful ladies I saw at the – ball."

It was only then, and it seemed extraordinary that he should have forgotten her, that the Marquis remembered Yasmin.

He recognised that this was the solution that Harry had suggested to him.

But he could honestly swear, although no one would believe him, that in his anxiety to find Zia and rescue her from Proteus, he had never given a thought to his own problem of Yasmin's allegations.

Now he knew that to marry Zia provided a genuine and uncontrived answer, but she must never become aware of the predicament that he had found himself in.

Because it was easier to convince her of how much he wanted her by kisses rather than words, he kissed her until they arrived back at Oke House.

As the horses came to a standstill, Zia cried,

"We are – home!"

"That is what it will be to you in the future," the Marquis said.

Then, as a footman opened the door of the carriage, Zia gave a little cry.

"What is it?" the Marquis asked.

"I have forgotten – I have forgotten to tell you what has happened to your horses!"

The door was open, but he did not move and she knew that he was listening to her.

"A man called 'Dixon' collected them from the riverbank and he is going to sell them."

There was a little tremor in Zia's voice because she knew how much it would upset the Marquis.

"The carriage," she added, "is to be taken to the – scrapyards."

"Thank you, my darling," the Marquis said quietly and climbed out of the carriage.

As he went into the house, he was not surprised to find that his secretary was waiting for him.

"I have now brought Miss Langley home, Barrett," he informed him, "and I have some important instructions to give you."

Mr. Barrett waited and the Marquis picked Zia up in his arms.

"I am carrying you, because I think you have been through enough for one night and the sooner you go to bed and dream of me the better!"

As he started up the stairs, she smiled up at him.

"I shall dream of – you and keep thanking you – over and over again in – my heart."

He did not answer, but carried her down the corridor and into her bedroom where the candles were lit.

There was no maid waiting, but the Marquis knew that he had only to pull the bell and she would come at once.

Very gently he put Zia down on the bed and then, holding her close against him, kissed her fiercely and possessively.

"You are mine!" he asserted. "We will talk about it tomorrow."

She looked at him, her eyes shining, and the Marquis thought that no woman could look more lovely or desirable.

With an effort he turned towards the door.

"Please – change your clothes at once," Zia cried. "I am afraid you may – catch a chill."

The Marquis was wearing just a shirt and a pair of tight-fitting black trousers.

They were not as wet as they had been, but they were still damp and Zia was being sensible.

"I will do as you tell me," he said as he went from the room, "which, of course, I will always do in the future!"

She laughed because she knew that it was she who would be obeying him, which was only what she wanted to do.

Then before she pulled the bell for her maid, she knelt down beside the bed.

Intensely she thanked God that she was safe and that Father Proteus could never hurt or threaten her again.

*

Zia had gone to sleep hoping that what hours were left of the night would pass quickly so that she could see the Marquis again.

In fact she slept peacefully until after noon.

When she eventually awoke, she rang for her breakfast, but before it could arrive Martha came into her room.

"You are back! Thank God you are back," she exclaimed. "Oh, Zia, we have all been so desperately concerned for you."

"I am back here safe thanks to his Lordship," Zia smiled, "but Martha, it was very very frightening!"

"It must have been," Martha agreed, "but we have all had strict instructions from his Lordship not to speak about it to you, to each other or to anybody else."

Zia was surprised and then when she thought it over she knew that the Marquis was wise.

If what had happened was talked about in the house, it would certainly soon be gossiped about by his smart friends and then the whole saga might appear in the newspapers.

'Father Proteus is dead,' she thought to herself, 'and so the sooner everybody – forgets about – him the better.'

Martha was, however, saying how worried everyone had been and before the Marquis arrived back Dobson had been in tears over the loss of his horses.

"I have just heard from Mr. Barrett," Martha went on, "that the horses and the carriage have been found and brought back to his Lordship's stables."

"I am so glad. I could not bear such magnificent animals to be hurt or sold to somebody who was cruel to them."

"They are safe," Martha smiled, "and now Mr. Barrett is thinking of taking me to the country next week to meet the lady who teaches at the estate school."

Because she sounded so excited about it, Zia changed the conversation from herself to Martha's new career and her new clothes.

All she really wanted, however, was to see the Marquis and, when she was dressed, she ran downstairs to find out if he was in the house.

She found him in the study and, when she opened the door, he was alone.

When he saw her, he rose from his desk and, moving to one side of it, held out his arms.

She ran towards him and he pulled her close to him and kissed her until they were both breathless.

"I was so afraid that you might have disappeared once again," he said in his deep voice.

"No, I am here and, when I woke up, I was sure that I was dreaming."

He kissed her again before he drew her towards the sofa and they both sat down.

"I have been making a lot of arrangements," he said. "First I went to see the Archbishop at Lambeth Palace and arrived there just as he was finishing his breakfast."

Zia looked at him wide-eyed and he explained,

"He has given me a Special Licence and that means, my lovely one, that we can go to Oke Castle and be married tomorrow, soon after we arrive, by my Chaplain."

"M-married!" Zia whispered.

"I want you with me both by day and by *night*," the Marquis said emphasising the last word.

Zia blushed and he thought that she looked as beautiful as dawn breaking over the sky.

"I am not going to wait a minute longer," he said. "Such unpredictable and extraordinary things happen to you that I am taking no more chances!"

"I want to marry you – I want to be – your wife," Zia whispered, "and it will be – very – very wonderful for me."

"And for me," the Marquis said.

He kissed her again and they only moved apart hastily when the door opened and Harry came in.

"Good morning," he said cheerily. "What has been happening? Zia never turned up at the party last night and you, Rayburn, failed to come riding with me this morning!"

"I am sorry, Harry, but I have been very busy. Firstly I want you to congratulate me, because Zia has promised to become my wife!"

"That is the best news I have heard in years!" Harry exclaimed. "Congratulations, old boy! And may I kiss your future bride?"

"Just this once," the Marquis agreed grudgingly, "but I don't expect you to make a habit of it!"

Harry laughed and kissed Zia on both cheeks.

Then, as if he could not resist it, the Marquis said,

"We will tell you what has happened, but you must never relate it to a living soul."

"I guessed that something was up," Harry said. "Give me a glass of champagne to fortify myself before I hear the tale."

He settled himself in an armchair with a glass of champagne in his hand and listened in astonishment to the story that the Marquis unfolded to him.

Only when it was all finished did he notice that his glass of champagne had remained untouched and he exclaimed,

"I just cannot believe it! All I have to say, Rayburn, is that I will never forgive you for not letting me in on the rescue party."

"I visited *The Unicorn* this morning," the Marquis remarked, "and I have never seen men so elated and pleased with themselves. Actually there were only three men to take to the Police Station where they have now been charged."

He glanced at Zia before he said a little hastily in case it should upset her,

"The man who called himself 'Father Proteus' was drowned and so was Saul, otherwise they would both have been charged with murder. However the others have not been charged with kidnapping but only with stealing valuable relics from the Convent."

"That was clever of you," Harry approved.

"They have been forced to reveal the whereabouts of the loot and they will get several years imprisonment for theft."

"So that disposes of everything that was menacing," Harry concluded.

His eyes met the Marquis's and they both knew that he was referring to Yasmin Caton.

They all had luncheon together and talked of everything except the horror that Zia had been put through.

After luncheon was over, the Marquis said,

"I still have a great deal to do and, as you will appreciate, my darling, the one person I must let into the secret that we are being married tomorrow night is the Prince of Wales. He would be extremely hurt if like everyone else he learnt of it the day after tomorrow in *The Gazette*."

"And we are going to the country," Zia said quickly.

She wanted to avoid meeting the beautiful ladies who had pursued the Marquis and who now would be upset because he was to be married.

Because they would be so jealous, she was sure that they would make subtle remarks to him about her that might make the Marquis love her less.

"We will leave soon after breakfast," the Marquis promised, "and now I want you to rest, as Grandmama is doing, until teatime."

The Dowager Marchioness had been thrilled to learn that her grandson had found Zia and that she was safe.

She had been so upset at what had happened that she had been advised to stay in bed, although she had said firmly that she would be down for dinner.

"I will look forward to seeing you then, Grandmama," the Marquis had said, "when I will tell you why I am the happiest man in the world."

When he left her, the Dowager Marchioness shed a few tears because she too was happy.

She had loved her grandson ever since he was a small boy and she had regretted bitterly as the years passed that, while there was a succession of beautiful women in his life, she had felt that with each *affaire de coeur* he became more and more cynical.

Now there was a happiness about him that she had not known for many years.

She felt that her prayers had been answered because Zia was exactly the right wife for him.

*

Because she was too excited and happy to be tired, Zia did not go to her room to rest.

Instead she went to the Marquis's study so that, when he returned, she would not miss a moment of his company.

She took a book from the case to read, but in fact she sat thinking how wonderful he was and that no one else could be more fortunate than herself because he loved her.

Then, when she was praying that she would never fail him, the door opened and she heard Carter the butler say,

"As you see, my Lady, I'm not deceiving you and his Lordship's not here."

"Then I will wait until he returns," a woman's voice replied.

"Very good, my Lady," Carter replied in a somewhat exasperated tone.

Zia was aware as he closed the door that she was no longer alone.

She had been sitting in a deep armchair beside the fireplace that was hidden from the door and now a little nervously she rose to her feet.

Standing by the desk was one of the most beautiful women she had ever seen.

Dressed in black she was nevertheless elegant with a bustle larger than anything that the Dowager Marchioness would have let her buy.

As Zia hesitated, wondering what she should say, the lady, who had been staring at a pile of letters, turned her head and saw her.

As she did so, she stiffened and there was no mistaking a hostile expression in her eyes.

"You are Zia Langley, I suppose," she began in a hard voice.

"Y-yes – I am," Zia answered, "and, if you are waiting for his Lordship, I am afraid he will be away for some time."

"Then I will speak to you," Lady Caton replied. "I have heard, although it may be untrue, that his Lordship intends to marry you."

"It is to be announced the day – after tomorrow."

Yasmin Caton gave a shrill scream.

"Then it *is* true! When I heard the rumour, I was sure that it must be a lie, because no man in the whole world could behave so despicably or so disgracefully! I only wish I could kill him for it!"

She spoke so violently that Zia felt intimidated.

"What – are you – saying? I-I don't – understand."

"Then let me tell you what you ought to know," the woman said moving a little nearer to her. "I am Lady Caton and the Marquis, with whom I suppose you fancy yourself to be in love, is a man of no principles and no decency. He is marrying you merely to escape from his responsibilities."

She seemed to spit the words at Zia, who instinctively moved back a step or two.

"I-I don't – understand what – you are saying."

"The truth is that Rayburn was in love with me. Because I believed his protestations of affection I became his mistress and he promised that, as soon as my husband died, he would marry me!"

Her voice sharpened as she went on,

"Now that I am free, he has run away from me and from the child I carry, which is his."

For a few seconds Zia did not understand what she was saying and then when she did she went very pale.

"You – you are – having a – baby?" she stammered.

"I suppose you can understand English?" Yasmin Caton snapped. "Yes, I am carrying the Marquis's child and are you prepared, you stupid little rich girl who will bore him stiff within a few weeks, to let him hide behind your skirts rather than do what is right and make my child legitimate?"

~168~

Zia could only stare at her and at the same time she was trembling.

Then suddenly, as if she wished to menace her, Yasmin Caton screamed,

"Go away! Leave him alone! He is mine do you understand? He is mine and however hard he tries to, I will not let him leave me!"

She spoke so violently that her voice echoed round the study walls.

With a cry like that of a small hurt animal, Zia turned and ran from the room.

She ran along the passage and across the hall, unaware that Carter and the footmen were staring at her, and up the stairs.

She rushed into her bedroom and shutting the door behind her flung herself down on the bed.

She was so shocked and so stunned by what she had just heard that she could not even cry.

She only lay there feeling as if the beautiful woman who had betrayed the Marquis had stabbed her in a thousand places and her whole body was bleeding to death.

'I have – to go – away,' she thought. 'She – is right and, if she is – bearing his – child, he must – marry her!'

Then she realised that she had nowhere to go.

There must be somewhere, but she could not think of it. Then almost as if she was being helped, she remembered the Marquis saying to Martha,

"If you want to go into a Convent, I will arrange with the Archbishop of Westminster Cathedral, that you go into the very best one there is."

A Convent!

It was the only refuge that she could think of at this moment. She was not a Roman Catholic, but she had told Father Anthony that she wished to become one. Any Convent would therefore take her and there would be no difficulties.

She took a hat from the wardrobe and, picking up her gloves and her handbag, she went down the stairs.

When she reached the hall, Carter was there and she asked him,

"Please will you call me a Hackney carriage?"

"A Hackney carriage, miss?" Carter exclaimed. "It'll take only a moment for me to send to the Mews for one of his Lordship's carriages."

"No, I want a Hackney carriage!" Zia said firmly.

"But, you can't be going out alone, miss?"

"I don't see why you should try to stop me," Zia answered, "and I don't think you have the right to do so."

Carter looked embarrassed.

He knew that something was wrong and after what had happened he could hardly believe that Miss Langley would again contemplate going driving alone.

"Now, listen, miss," he said in the kindly tones of an old family servant, "I know that his Lordship would not want you to go alone in a public vehicle when our horses and coachmen are available in the Mews."

"I have – to go – *I have to*!" Zia replied desperately.

"I think, miss, that first you should speak to Mr. Barrett."

Zia felt as if once again she was being confined against her will.

As it was a warm and sunny day, the front door was open and, without saying another word, she passed Carter, running down the steps and out through the short drive into Park Lane.

Carter stood staring after her in astonishment.

Then he said to one of the footmen, who he thought was more sensible than the others,

"Follow Miss Langley, James, and don't let her out of your sight. If she takes a Hackney carriage, find another one and follow her. Do you understand?"

"Yes, Mr. Carter!"

Carter put his hand into his pocket, took out the first coins he found in it and gave them to the boy.

"Hurry now, *hurry!*" he said urgently. "And don't lose her, whatever you do!"

As James ran into Park Lane, Carter walked so quickly that he too was almost running to Mr. Barrett's office.

*

Zia found a Hackney carriage that was for hire almost immediately and told the driver to take her to Westminster Cathedral.

As it was a warm day, the hood was down, but to Zia there was no sunshine, only an impenetrable darkness.

She was driven very much more slowly than she would have been behind the Marquis's spirited and well-bred horses.

It was, however, not very far to Westminster Cathedral and all the time she was fighting back her tears.

She was determined to speak sensibly to the Cardinal so that he would understand her anxiety to enter into a Convent immediately.

'I shall never – love anyone – else,' she told herself miserably, 'so how can I – stay in the world when I might see – him with his – wife and – his children?'

She closed her eyes feeling the pain that it gave her.

It was an agony to think that perhaps his love for her had been false and, as Lady Caton had claimed, he was merely trying to evade his responsibilities.

'How can I – live without – him?' she asked the ceiling despairingly.

She wished that last night she had been able to throw herself into the River Thames and be drowned, as Father Proteus had been.

When she reached Westminster Cathedral, she paid off the Hackney Carriage and walked into the huge Basilica.

There was a strong scent of incense and hundreds of candles were flickering in the side Chapels.

She genuflected and stood for a moment looking at the High Altar and, then seeing a man who looked like a Verger, she went up to him and said,

"I wish to see His Eminence the Cardinal. Is that possible?"

Her appearance obviously impressed him for without hesitation the Verger replied,

"I'm not certain, madam, if His Eminence is available, but Monseigneur St. Ives is, I know in the Cathedral and perhaps you would speak with him?"

"Thank you very much," Zia answered.

She was led down a side aisle and behind the Altar until the man who was leading her asked her to wait a moment outside a closed door.

She stood there feeling more numb than anything else.

It was as if the agony she felt at first after she had listened to the Marquis's visitor had stunned her.

Now she was feeling almost detached from herself.

The door in front of her opened and the Verger who had escorted her there said,

"The Monseigneur will see you now, madam."

Zia walked forward and found that she was in a small room rather like an office.

There were many religious books on a number of shelves and the Monseigneur, a kindly-looking elderly man, was sitting at a desk.

As she entered he rose and she curtseyed to him as she had done when she was in the Convent to Father Anthony and indeed later to Father Proteus.

"You wanted to see me?" the Monseigneur asked gently, holding out his hand.

"I-I have a – request to make, Monseigneur," Zia replied.

He indicated a chair on the other side of the desk and they both sat down.

"Now what can I do for you?" the Monseigneur enquired.

Zia drew in her breath.

"I want to – become a Roman Catholic – and enter a Convent. I am – wealthy – so that I can endow any Convent that will – receive me."

"You have thought this over carefully?" the Monseigneur asked her after a slight pause.

"Yes – and I have already had some – instruction at the Convent I attended in Cornwall."

"What is its name?"

"The Convent of the Holy Thorn," Zia replied to him. "It was partly a school – and Father Anthony who was – in charge is very ill – and it is – unlikely he will recover."

"I have heard of this Convent," the Monseigneur remarked.

"I have been there for the last two years," Zia explained, "but then I was – persuaded to – try to live in the – Social world, but now – I know it is not for me."

As she spoke, she could not prevent the agony she was feeling sounding in her voice.

The Monseigneur bent forward to say,

"I think you are unhappy, my child. Is this the reason why you wish to enter a Convent?"

Because it was impossible for Zia to speak, she nodded her head and he said gently,

"Unhappiness is not always the best reason for dedicating your life to God. I would like you to think over the possibility of remaining in the Social world that you belong to for a little while longer before you make any hasty decision that will so greatly affect your whole life."

"I have – made my – decision," Zia answered. "Please take me – take me – now!"

She looked at the Monseigneur and her eyes filled with tears.

Then, as he hesitated, obviously feeling for words, the door behind him opened and the same Verger who had escorted Zia announced,

"A gentleman to see you, Monseigneur."

Zia did not look round, but she heard footsteps behind her and to her astonishment a deep voice said,

"Zia! How could you do anything so foolish?"

Zia still did not turn her head.

Instead she put her hands over her eyes and could not stop herself from crying.

The Marquis looked down at her and then he said,

"You must forgive me, Monseigneur. I am the Marquis of Okehampton. I saw my Ward driving alone in a Hackney carriage past Buckingham Palace and I then followed her here, knowing that there must be something wrong."

"I think there is," Monseigneur St. Ives answered, "and I suggest, my Lord, that I leave you two alone together to discuss your differences. Afterwards, if you or the young lady wishes to see me, I will be available."

"You are very kind," the Marquis said, "and I am extremely grateful."

Immediately the Monseigneur went from the room closing the door behind him and the Marquis sat down in a chair that was beside Zia's.

"Now, tell me what has happened?" he asked gently. "What is wrong? I could hardly believe it possible when I saw you driving alone."

Zia did not reply and after a moment he said,

"Why did you come here?"

"I – want to – enter a – Convent!" Zia murmured.

"And leave me?"

"Y-yes."

The monosyllable was hardly audible, but the Marquis heard it and after a moment he said,

"I thought you loved me!"

"I do – *I do*!" Zia sobbed. "But you belong to – her and – I cannot – stay in a world – where I might – see you with somebody else as your – w-wife."

The Marquis stiffened.

Then he said,

"Stop crying, my darling, and tell me exactly what has happened and why it has upset you."

Zia did not answer nor did she take her hands from her eyes, but she was no longer crying.

Very gently the Marquis bent forward to pull her hands from her face.

Her cheeks were stained with tears, her long eyelashes were wet and, when she looked at him, he saw the pain and agony in her eyes.

It made him go down on one knee beside her and put his arms round her shoulders.

"What has happened, my darling, my precious little love?"

He could feel Zia trembling and she looked down.

Then in a voice he could hardly hear she stammered,

"The – Lady said – she was – carrying your – baby – and you had promised to – marry her."

The Marquis was very still.

And then he said,

"Look at me, my precious, I want you to look at me."

Slowly she raised her eyes to his and, when she had done so, he said,

"We are in a Holy place, the House of God, and I swear to you by everything I hold sacred, on the memory of my mother whom I loved as you loved yours, that no woman, including the one who spoke to you, has ever had a child by me."

Zia stared at him.

"You have to believe me," he went on, "because I think that your instinct and your love for me would tell you if I was lying, just as it will also make you know that I am telling you the truth."

He saw a little flicker of light in Zia's eyes before she said,

"Then – why – why should – she say such a – thing?"

"Because she had made up her mind to marry me, even while her husband was still living."

"But – you don't – want to – m-marry her?"

"I have never wanted to marry any woman, except you!" the Marquis asserted truthfully.

"Then I don't – understand – why – ?"

"Listen to me, my precious. I will not pretend to you that there has not been a number of women in my life. I am a man and if a beautiful woman wishes to honour me by giving herself to me, I would be inhuman if I did not accept such favours."

He saw that Zia was listening and he carried on,

"But you are intelligent enough to understand that a man may desire a woman because she is beautiful and that what he feels for her is an appreciation such as he would feel for a beautiful flower or the joy that is expressed in music or the warmth of the sun."

He felt Zia relax a little as he continued,

"But, while it can be a delightful sensation, it is not real love, the love that I have for you, my dearest heart, and that I believe you have for me. What we have found together is the love that comes from God, the love a man has for the one special woman in his life, who is actually the other half of himself."

He drew Zia a little closer to him.

"It is the very special love that your father had for your mother and my father had for mine. It is the love that is Divine and which could never ever be spoilt by lies, deception or treachery."

Zia made a little murmur and the Marquis went on,

"Just as Father Proteus was a bad man, so the woman you have just met is bad beneath the beauty of her face. We simply have to forget them both."

"But – suppose," Zia said in a very small voice, "she – tries to – hurt you?"

"That she has done already by upsetting you," the Marquis said. "I had no idea, when her husband has not yet been buried, that she would come to my house or that you would see her and she would tell you such a lie."

There was silence between them.

Then Zia said,

"I am – sorry – forgive me – I should have – trusted – you."

"That is what I want you to do," the Marquis said, "and you must forgive me – that I have sinned in the past, which I can swear to you here in the Cathedral, is something I shall never do in the future."

Zia gave a little sob.

"I love you – *I love – you*!" she whispered, "but when I – came here – I-I wanted to – d-die!"

"And now we both want to live. And I want you to come home for you have to choose your Wedding gown that you will become my wife in tomorrow."

As he spoke, he drew Zia to her feet.

"I love you with all my heart and all my soul," he said. "That, my darling, is something I have never said to any other woman for it would not have been true."

"And – I love – you!" Zia whispered. "You fill the – whole world – the sky and the sea – and I know, if I – lost you, I would have – nothing – nothing at all."

"You will never lose me," the Marquis vowed.

She thought that he would kiss her.

But, as if he was thinking of the Holy place they were in, he raised her hands to his lips and kissed first one and then the other.

Then he drew her towards the door.

When they reached it, they saw on duty outside the Verger who had brought the Marquis to Monseigneur St. Ives's study.

"May I speak to the Monseigneur again for a moment?" the Marquis enquired.

"I regret, sir, the Monseigneur is presently in the Confessional, but he asked me to tell you that he would pray for you."

"Will you thank the Monseigneur," the Marquis said, "and say that I will be sending him a thank-offering."

The Marquis walked down the aisle with Zia, and as they did so she felt as if the Saints in the Chapels they passed were giving them a special Blessing.

Then they were outside in the sunshine and she saw the Marquis's phaeton drawn by two horses that were being held by a groom.

They drove back the way that Zia had come past Buckingham Palace.

They did not speak, but Zia felt as though the sun had never been brighter and it seemed to envelop them with an aura of happiness.

When they arrived back at Oke House, Zia was aware that there was an expression of relief on Carter's face as he saw that she was with the Marquis.

As she ran up to her bedroom to take off her hat, Carter informed the Marquis in a low voice what had occurred and how anxious he had been.

"By sheer chance, I saw Miss Langley driving past Buckingham Palace, where I had been to see His Royal Highness, who was holding an Investiture," the Marquis explained. "However, it was sensible and very intelligent of you, Carter, to have sent someone after her. But then I know that I can always rely on you."

Carter was now beaming.

Then the Marquis asked,

"Is Lady Caton still here?"

"She left fifteen minutes ago, my Lord, having waited for nearly an hour."

"If she calls again," the Marquis ordered firmly, "I am not at home!"

"I had no idea that Miss Langley was in the study, my Lord."

"I realise that, but don't make another mistake before we leave tomorrow morning for The Castle and say nothing of all this to her Ladyship."

"No, of course not, my Lord. It would only upset her."

The Marquis wanted to say that it had upset him, but by the mercy of God everything was now all right.

Then, as if he could not wait another minute to see Zia, he gave orders,

"We will have tea in the drawing room."

"Very good, my Lord."

He went upstairs to wait for Zia to come from her bedroom.

*

There was so much that Zia wanted to see in The Castle when they arrived after stopping on the way for luncheon, but the Marquis insisted firmly that she was to rest.

They were to be married at five o'clock and he sent her to her bedroom until then.

She guessed that one of his reasons was that he wished to see that the Private Chapel was filled with flowers and later she found that she had not been mistaken.

It was a small but very beautiful Chapel that had been built at the same time as The Castle and very few alterations had been made to it over the years.

Only the Marquis, she thought, could have contrived that it was filled with Arum lilies and their sublime fragrance scented the air.

It was the perfect background for her white gown that had arrived just before they left London and had been ordered by the Marquis almost from the moment that he had asked her to be his wife.

"How could you have been so marvellous in planning everything – so cleverly?" she asked him as they drove through the beautiful countryside towards The Castle.

"I want everything in your life to be perfect, as perfect, my precious, as our love."

"That is so – perfect that there are no – words to – describe it," Zia said softly.

It was what the Marquis thought too.

Harry, who was to be his Best Man, had said to him last night after dinner,

"You are marrying exactly the right woman in taking Zia as your wife."

"I love her!" the Marquis said fiercely.

He was afraid that Harry was still thinking that he was marrying her purely to be rid of Yasmin.

"I know that, Rayburn, and I have never seen you looking so happy or so pleased with yourself!"

The Marquis laughed.

He knew it was true that he was happy.

He also was pleased to believe that he had been clever enough to find the one woman in the world who he was sure was different from anyone else.

He had taken Zia to The Castle alone and Harry had arranged to stay with friends who lived only about two miles away.

"You realise," he said, "that everyone will want to tear my eyes out if I am the only guest at your marriage? They will all be expecting a big 'slap-up' feast with the Prince of Wales present and at least a dozen bridesmaids."

"Then they will be disappointed. This is exactly the sort of Wedding that I have always wanted, but thought I would never be lucky enough to have."

"What you are really saying is that it is the sort of Wedding that Zia wants too," Harry remarked.

"Of course," the Marquis agreed. "After all she has been through, I am not having her upset by women being spiteful or men making eyes at her."

Harry laughed.

"She is so beautiful that you will be kept busy fending off men like Charles who will find her irresistible."

"I know that," the Marquis agreed, "but we are going to spend most of our time in the country and men like Charles will not be amongst our guests!"

The Marquis paused.

Then he said,

"As a matter of fact, I do *not* intend to have any guests for a long time. I want Zia all to myself."

The way he spoke made Harry gaze at him enviously. It was indeed the sort of marriage he wanted himself if he ever found a woman he wished to marry.

But that could be said of every man who, like Lord Charles Fane, flitted from boudoir to boudoir inevitably to be bored and disappointed.

*

As the Marquis and Zia knelt side by side for the final Blessing from the Chaplain, they were holding hands.

It seemed to them that the vibrations that they felt emanating from within themselves were like a Divine Light.

They left the Chapel and, without speaking to anyone, as the Marquis had arranged, they went up to Zia's bedroom, which had been his mother's.

The Marquis closed the door and then to Zia's surprise he did not take her in his arms, but drew her to the window.

They stood looking out at the garden, the lake that lay beyond it and the great oak trees in the Park.

Beyond that there was a vista over the woods that eventually led to the sea.

For a moment the Marquis did not speak.

Then he said,

"This is my world, my precious, which is now yours. I think we will both love it, rule over it and try to give everyone who lives in it the same happiness that we have ourselves."

Zia gave a little exclamation and moved closer to him.

"Only – you, darling Rayburn could – think like that."

"It is the way you have taught me to think," he answered, "but it has been there in my heart, although I have never been able to express it until now."

He put his arms round her and there was no longer any need for words.

*

A long time later when the sun was sinking and the rooks were going to roost in the trees, the Marquis said,

"I am wondering, my darling glorious wife, why you are so different from any woman I have ever known before."

"Am I – so different?" Zia asked. "You are so – wonderful – so utterly and completely – marvellous that when you made love to me I was – just a little afraid – as it was so new to me – that you would not – feel the same as I did."

"I felt all that you felt and more," the Marquis said, "and once again I am being truthful when I tell you that never has anything been so perfect or so glorious as loving you."

Zia gave a little cry.

"That is exactly what I wanted you to say – and please, darling, never grow bored with – loving me."

"How could I be bored with anything that seems to carry me up to the Heaven that we believe in and which makes me feel as if I hold an enchanting angel in my arms."

He bent over Zia and moved the softness of her hair back from her oval forehead.

"You are very beautiful," he said, "but so are other women. What is it about you that is so different?"

"Tell me – please tell me what it is."

"I know the answer. It is because you are so good and I have known few really good women in my life!"

"I am sure – that is not – true, but I want you to think that I am."

"You are good, as my mother was," the Marquis said. "Until now I have never found anyone who could ever mean what she meant to me, but now there is you and in many ways you are very like her."

"I am – thrilled that you – should think – so," Zia murmured.

"I know, my beautiful little wife, that you are good in your heart and in your soul and that is what I want you to be and nothing shall ever spoil you."

The Marquis paused before he said in a different tone,

"If any man attempted to do so, I swear I would kill him!"

His voice just seemed to ring out round the room and then he was kissing Zia fiercely, demandingly and possessively.

His lips almost hurt her and yet she was not afraid.

She knew that this feeling of possessiveness was very much part of their love and in fact love was not the soft, gentle sentimental thing she had thought it to be.

It was strong, vibrant, often violent, often disruptive and at the same time invincible and irresistible.

She knew it was love that had made the Marquis strong and clever enough to fight for her and to save her from Proteus.

It was the love that in the future would enable them to battle against any obstacles or difficulties for, of course, there would be some in their lives.

But he would always be the victor, always the conqueror, simply because his love gave him the strength to overcome evil and anything that was wrong or wicked,

The Marquis's kisses became more demanding and she saw that there was a fire in his eyes.

There was also a fire within him that made her know that, while he worshipped her, he also desired her as a woman.

She could feel the same fire within herself and now it was flickering with the flames.

"I want you! My darling, I want you!" the Marquis sighed,

"I am – yours!" Zia murmured.

"Give me yourself, love me, for only God knows how much I really love you."

"I – love you – *I love – you*!"

The words seemed to burn with an intensity within them both.

Then, as the Marquis made Zia his, they were swept together into the burning heart of the sun.

The glory of their love enveloped them both with the Divine Light that comes from God, which is Life itself and is Eternal.

OTHER BOOKS IN THIS SERIES

The Barbara Cartland Eternal Collection is the unique opportunity to collect all five hundred of the timeless beautiful romantic novels written by the world's most celebrated and enduring romantic author.

Named the Eternal Collection because Barbara's inspiring stories of pure love, just the same as love itself, the books will be published on the internet at the rate of four titles per month until all five hundred are available.

The Eternal Collection, classic pure romance available worldwide for all time.

1. Elizabethan Lover
2. The Little Pretender
3. A Ghost in Monte Carlo
4. A Duel of Hearts
5. The Saint and the Sinner
6. The Penniless Peer
7. The Proud Princess
8. The Dare-Devil Duke
9. Diona and a Dalmatian
10. A Shaft of Sunlight
11. Lies for Love
12. Love and Lucia
13. Love and the Loathsome Leopard
14. Beauty or Brains
15. The Temptation of Torilla
16. The Goddess and the Gaiety Girl
17. Fragrant Flower
18. Look, Listen and Love
19. The Duke and the Preacher's Daughter
20. A Kiss For The King
21. The Mysterious Maid-Servant
22. Lucky Logan Finds Love
23. The Wings of Ecstasy
24. Mission to Monte Carlo
25. Revenge of the Heart
26. The Unbreakable Spell
27. Never Laugh at Love
28. Bride to a Brigand
29. Lucifer and the Angel
30. Journey to a Star
31. Solita and the Spies
32. The Chieftain without a Heart
33. No Escape from Love
34. Dollars for the Duke
35. Pure and Untouched
36. Secrets
37. Fire in the Blood
38. Love, Lies and Marriage
39. The Ghost who fell in love
40. Hungry for Love
41. The wild cry of love
42. The blue eyed witch
43. The Punishment of a Vixen
44. The Secret of the Glen

45. Bride to The King
46. For All Eternity
47. A King in Love
48. A Marriage Made in Heaven
49. Who Can Deny Love?
50. Riding to The Moon
51. Wish for Love
52. Dancing on a Rainbow
53. Gypsy Magic
54. Love in the Clouds
55. Count the Stars
56. White Lilac
57. Too Precious to Lose
58. The Devil Defeated
59. An Angel Runs Away
60. The Duchess Disappeared
61. The Pretty Horse-breakers
62. The Prisoner of Love
63. Ola and the Sea Wolf
64. The Castle made for Love
65. A Heart is Stolen
66. The Love Pirate
67. As Eagles Fly
68. The Magic of Love
69. Love Leaves at Midnight
70. A Witch's Spell
71. Love Comes West
72. The Impetuous Duchess
73. A Tangled Web
74. Love Lifts the Curse
75. Saved By A Saint
76. Love is Dangerous
77. The Poor Governess
78. The Peril and the Prince
79. A Very Unusual Wife
80. Say Yes Samantha
81. Punished with love
82. A Royal Rebuke
83. The Husband Hunters
84. Signpost To Love
85. Love Forbidden
86. Gift of the Gods

87. The Outrageous Lady
88. The Slaves of Love
89. The Disgraceful Duke
90. The Unwanted Wedding
91. Lord Ravenscar's Revenge
92. From Hate to Love
93. A Very Naughty Angel
94. The Innocent Imposter
95. A Rebel Princess
96. A Wish Come True
97. Haunted
98. Passions In The Sand
99. Little White Doves of Love
100. A Portrait of Love
101. The Enchanted Waltz
102. Alone and Afraid
103. The Call of the Highlands
104. The Glittering Lights
105. An Angel in Hell
106. Only a Dream
107. A Nightingale Sang
108. Pride and the Poor Princess
109. Stars in my Heart
110. The Fire of Love
111. A Dream from the Night
112. Sweet Enchantress
113. The Kiss of the Devil
114. Fascination in France
115. Love Runs in
116. Lost Enchantment
117. Love is Innocent
118. The Love Trap
119. No Darkness for Love
120. Kiss from a Stranger
121. The Flame Is Love
122. A Touch Of Love
123. The Dangerous Dandy
124. In Love In Lucca
125. The Karma of Love
126. Magic from the Heart
127. Paradise Found
128. Only Love

129. A Duel with Destiny
130. The Heart of the Clan
131. The Ruthless Rake
132. Revenge Is Sweet
133. Fire on the Snow
134. A Revolution of Love
135. Love at the Helm
136. Listen to Love
137. Love Casts out Fear
138. The Devilish Deception
139. Riding in the Sky
140. The Wonderful Dream
141. This Time it's Love
142. The River of Love
143. A Gentleman in Love
144. The Island of Love
145. Miracle for a Madonna
146. The Storms of Love
147. The Prince and the Pekingese
148. The Golden Cage
149. Theresa and a Tiger
150. The Goddess of Love
151. Alone in Paris
152. The Earl Rings a Belle
153. The Runaway Heart
154. From Hell to Heaven
155. Love in the Ruins
156. Crowned with Love
157. Love is a Maze
158. Hidden by Love
159. Love Is The Key
160. A Miracle In Music
161. The Race For Love
162. Call of The Heart
163. The Curse of the Clan
164. Saved by Love
165. The Tears of Love
166. Winged Magic
167. Born of Love
168. Love Holds the Cards
169. A Chieftain Finds Love
170. The Horizons of Love
171. The Marquis Wins
172. A Duke in Danger
173. Warned by a Ghost
174. Forced to Marry
175. Sweet Adventure
176. Love is a Gamble
177. Love on the Wind
178. Looking for Love
179. Love is the Enemy
180. The Passion and the Flower
181. The Reluctant Bride
182. Safe in Paradise
183. The Temple of Love
184. Love at First Sight
185. The Scots Never Forget
186. The Golden Gondola
187. No Time for Love
188. Love in the Moon
189. A Hazard of Hearts
190. Just Fate
191. The Kiss of Paris
192. Little Tongues of Fire
193. Love under Fire
194. The Magnificent Marriage
195. Moon over Eden
196. The Dream and The Glory
197. A Victory for Love
198. A Princess in Distress
199. A Gamble with Hearts
200. Love strikes a Devil
201. In the arms of Love
202. Love in the Dark
203. Love Wins
204. The Marquis Who Hated Women
205. Love is Invincible
206. Love Climbs in
207. The Queen Saves the King
208. The Duke Comes Home